THE SEEDS OF KAIN

GEORGE WILLIAM BELL

Dedicated to dearest Vicky,
a sweet girl,
who grew on good soil

Disclaimer

Any resemblance to any person living or dead is purely coincidental.

ISBN: 978-1-9164272-0-4

Published by: Grosvenor Artist Management

www.grosvenorartistmanagement.com

Prologue

The bullet blew the life out of the baby vulture….young and vulnerable, now dead. The parents flew around in anguish as the white man re-loaded his gun. He shot again….the second baby vulture was sprayed to the wind. The man laughed and left. The birds flew to the branch of the live oak and sat.

Snake Kain was a man with evil in him….the birds would remember him.

Just as seeds

Scattered to air

We must grow

In whatever soil

We land in.

Chapter 1

"Git here," he said. "Stand there," he said. He snatched me up sudden like that, by the shirt front, stretched me up till my heels lifted up. "Prissy looking runt 'aint you Northern boy, how old did you say you was?" "Fifteen," I uttered out. This was my first solid knowledge of the man known as Snake Kain.

I stood after that, shocked after that; I stared wild after that, terrified. He was a violent man this Snake Kain, this man whose gut rose and fell. He breathed on me, his breath was a bad smell on me.... it was beer, I know it was that, but there was some worse bad smell in it.... the smell of a man rotting.

"This 'ere's a hell place you're at Northern boy".... it looked like a hell place it did.... all bare dirt, and further as far as sight could get, rusting automobiles under the sun.... "Where you're at boy is Caloosahatchee Wreckers and Reclaimers." He said it proud, with all his face and gut he said it.

I was on the edge of a faint just then, on account of that breath, on account of being shocked sick that much, on account of raw grief, raw from my Mother's funeral back in Ohio. I had spent away three days on train and bus to get to this. Snake Kain tilted himself to me, said....

"Hope you've brought no bent Ohia traits with you boy…. she'll have her will with you…. straighten you out just as if you was a bent clothes hanger…."

'She' I was to find out was Miss Lorraine.

A screen door clattered back just then, she stood side-on, had gripped in her hand a saw-edged knife. "Mr Kain! WHERE'R YOU AT….? GIT yourself here, AND NOW!" There stood Miss Lorraine. I was raised with stories of this high-bred porcelain Southern lady, but her body was spoiled by fat, she had no waist on her. In honest truth, could this be her, the wife of Snake Kain? When she saw me, she ran at me…. with a 'Southern yell' she ran. Still with a grip on that saw-edge knife behind my back, she gave a hug, enough to snap three ribs, she held me like that, in a grip. I felt ill I did, and the sight past her neck of ghastly twisted broken automobiles, and nowhere to look but to see them, brought me to the swallowing stage of putting something off. "This knife's dull Mr Kain".... she said, letting her grip off me…. "Dull enough to ride bareback on Mr Kain. Give it a licking with that file of yours, and don't take the day over it…. I'll see to the boy. Well Lafe, we'll soon get you SOUTHERNIZED and CIVILISED!" just at that word, I hurled out my whole bus station meal onto the dry Florida dirt…. "LORD preserve us!" She yelped hands to heaven, she directed my bent frame at arm's length toward the house, exclaiming, "I never expected a flinging-up as an introduction!" In the kitchen I was dosed, next to the sink, apron tied rough round my neck in bib fashion. Without water, without question, I was sent upstairs, first right, still wearing the bib, holding a bowl. The room was yellow, the bed narrow, after a piece of time the ceiling faded off…. I escaped in sleep.

Chapter 2

A sound jolted me awake. Out from a groan came words….
"I'll smash that gadam Yankee runts bones…." for an endless
space of black no sound. I lay crushed by heat, new clothes
wet, throat acid. In that blank I saw my mother silent in
the earth, far from here, cold. I thought how much warmer
she was in the earth and in me, than these living dead here.
There was a low voice, a woman's voice, "We'll get free of
him soon enough…. let it go till a decent spell, he'll be glad
to settle it then. All we have to do is make his life not too
comfortable." Now the strangest voice made words, a gassy
voice, an underwater voice, but dry too; there were gaps
between words, but the words themselves I could not get.
After a bit, quiet fell in, I fell back into sleep.

A piece of sunlight was across me. The mixed smell of
cooking bacon and mildew from the mattress caused a new
smell. I thought myself glad I was not strangled dead in the
night, or not so glad, for that apron Miss Lorraine had fixed
on me so violently had twisted itself to my back, when I
stood, it hung like a cape.

Nervous, I made my way downstairs. I had my mind strong
made up, I would run from this place…. I was thrown off
the thought by a stare. An old man sat tough at the kitchen
table, arms wide, with a grip at each table edge…. as if to
own the whole of everything. A voice came that seemed
not from him, that same gassy underwater voice I heard
last night, it ran out dry to a whisper. "Set yourself…. for
some…. grits and…. bacon boy." He kept his hard eye on
me. This was the man I was to know as Old Mr Kain, a man
my father had spoken of when he talked of the Southern

Kains, and Snake's father. I was about to sit at the far other end of the table from him. "No boy," he pointed, getting breath, "That's Miss Lorraine's place. Your place…. is to the…. side boy…. same as…. Snake's is…. to the opposite." I was glad Snake Kain was not there.

At the end of the kitchen, Miss Lorraine was bossing some bacon round an iron fry pan. She banged out three plates of white glue material, threw some bacon on with it, and before anything, took off her winged eye glasses, which, with fierce rubbing, she washed free of splatters. "Mr Snake had an argument with your suitcase last night," she said, as she dumped the plates in front of her two eaters. "Hold up now you two heathens." Old Kain lowered his fork…. "No eating without grace." She stabbed off some words that took in eat and Lord and sat. "As I said, Mr Snake went full length over your little suitcase last evening. I'd left it for you on the landing. It's only one of those cheap cardboard arrangements, a good jumping on it from the inside'll see it right."

We ate in silence. I ate the bacon, but the white glue, that they were meantime shovelling down, I left. "Do my eyes lie?" said Miss Lorraine half getting off her chair. "I… I don't know what it is." "Your education has fallen bad short on the food side boy; why 'Dixie Lillie,' haven't you never heard of 'Dixie Lilly' grits boy?…. grits is corn…. corn put in lye to get the skins off, corn dried and coarse ground…. that's what grits is; if its cooked right, it's like this. Bi' the looks of you, you're in bad need of it. Here, here's a lump more butter on it…. now get it down, or I'll think your flinging up last evening was the coming on of some bad thing…. cause for more dosing!" So saying, she gave an example of 'getting it down' by getting down half a plate full. But it wasn't the pile of glue on its own that put me off. I had seen something on the old man's neck, a flap, it moved at every breath take. Could it be he was breathing out of his NECK?

There was a noise. Mr Snake Kain shuffled, stood, grabbed the kitchen door upright; vivid bad was the pain told by his eyes, for he was a man in a state of hurting. "Just alive again is it?" Miss Lorraine jabbed, her neck raised, twisted his direction… "No breakfast for those who do the deadly sin…. there is such a thing as liquid gluttony Mr Kain!" She jarred back her chair legs, as a form of hitting him, stood. Snake Kain flinched, speeded up his moving past her, went stiff-legged out the front door. As the screen door slammed, she muttered, "Useless Lummox," slopped out more glue, which I had to cover my plate to say 'no' to.

"Done are you? …. I have it in mind to sort you out some more fittin' kit than that Sunday get-up you have on…. go out…. go introduce yourself to the palm trees. I have cleaning troubles to get on with…. and…. boy, if that old black is out there, name of Eli, tell him to rouse Mr Snake Kain, and that Miss Lorraine ordered it. There's a lesson in it for you boy…. go look…. look at Proverbs, Chapter 23, verse 21 'For the drunkard and the glutton shall come to poverty, and drowsiness shall cloth a man with rags.'"

As the screen door flung back behind me, the sun fired off a thousand windshields, off a thousand dead cars baking, to the horizon. Two good minutes went till I could see. A figure was bent over the insides of an automobile. I walked there, he kept working. "Are you Eli?" I said. "That's me," he looked off his work. "You're the Northern relation I've heard about…. I bet." He had his hands still in the engine, like a surgeon, for Eli had long and thin fingers. "I would say 'Welcome to the Caloosahatchee Wreckers,' but it ain't much of a place to be welcomed to boy. We don't grow nothing on this ten acres here but rust. Let me look at you," he smiled; his smile was made of overlapped teeth and teeth gone, but it was good and warm, the first smile I had seen in this place. I told Eli Miss Lorraine's orders, he digested them a bit, said, "I hate this alarm-clock job… most of any job, I hate it. We'll give Mr Snake a spell more, maybe it'll improve his bile."

Eli worked on, said no more except in a low voice…. "It's better to dwell in a corner of the housetop, than with a brawling woman in a wide house."

After a gap of time, Eli wiped off his hands, said, "One of the few advantages boy, of being black in this place… engine grease don't show much. We'd better swallow down hard boy…. git over to wake 'His Lordship'." Eli limped as we walked across the clearing. The tired uneven earth barren of cars, was a mix-up of dust and oil and nuts and bolts. There was a big wood platform set at the height of a man, with steps up. On this platform stood two young black men, no shirts, each behind a giant wood bin. They elbow nudged each other, followed Eli and I with their eyes, said not a word. A massive metal building, windowless, stood behind these two workers, on the door the grimed words 'Parts Shed', with the 'S' in shed written backwards.

Eli peered in, opening the door a crack, beckoned me follow, finger to lips. Inside the dim huge building, we stood under a sky of car bits hanging, labels hanging. The floor was a copy of that above, a litter of reclaimed parts, all this in a thick hot air of engine oil. Eli whispered, "Watch out, there's not much foot room through." By the wall, we saw him, Snake Kain, sprawled on an army camping cot, his big gut rising, falling. In back of him, tacked upright to the wall were five rattlesnake skins, one near tall as a man and a half. There was that same smell of rot breathed yesterday. A long revolver lay in the crooked angle of his arm like a teddy bear. "Oh Lord, he 'as that gun," whispered Eli. "I don't like to git too close-in when he's like this, and with that gun, he's like a snake his-self. Get in back of the counter, it's good and thick… ready to duck down now boy" …. my heart was in my neck. "Mr Kain sir…. Mr Kain!!" yelled Eli, "Miss Lorraine ordered you woke." Snake Kain stirred, snorted, grabbed at the gun, we ducked.

From behind the counter we heard him fumble, ready the gun. "Leave me be, 'oor I'll blast you gone," he shouted.

"It's Eli, and the relation boy.... Miss Lorraine ordered...."
"Miss Lorraine ordered you as a vengeance, you old black bastard, I'll have your pelt tacked up alongside 'o these, that'll show the bitch. Go.... go leave me, can't you see I'm in a mess of pain." "But Miss Lorraine...." "A poxilation on Miss Lorraine, git or I'll blast you gone, I will fire." He threw a brake caliper at us wielded the gun our direction. We were quick out.

Outside the light was scalding. "Faster out than two greased pigs!" yelled the two black workers rolling in laughter-fits on their platform above, while I tried to pretend I hadn't just almost messed my pants. Eli said, "We be lucky boy, last time he threw a starter motor; if I'd had any idea he had that revolver loose, I'd have never gone in, or taken you neither boy." At that, the door flung back, Snake Kain stood, swaying forward to back. He fired in the air, it left a ringing in the air.... "You sons of bitches.... SHUT UP!" he slammed that door behind himself. A stunned moment went, Eli said, "For someone who don't like noise, he sure do make a lot his-self." "Hadn't we better hush our voices Eli?" "Naa boy, when you gets threats once or twice in a day every day like we do, you gets to where you're thick to it.... He'll likely round his-self off with a couple more Papst Blue Ribbon specials, once he's got that down his neck, he'll sleep his headache off."

One of the tough looking boys behind the bins shouted down.... "Where you from boy?" "Ohio," I said, quiet as I could. "You sure is the picture of northern money!" Eli looked me over, smiled, "You'll be good for a mosquito scarer in that get-up" he said "Don't you have nothing rough to throw on them shoulders?" I told him of Miss Lorraine's clothing plans. "You'd better eat good, and eat fast boy, she'll likely try to fit you out in one of Snake's old overalls. Pity you hadn't a twin you could share.... one in each leg!"

It was true, when I got back Miss Lorraine was churning her deep arm in a bin of rags. She fished up a ghastly big pair of overalls, worn thin at the gut place, with plenty of gut room. Gritting a tape-measure by her teeth, she moved me about as if I was a thing. She took near fifty measurements. Now she got cutting, cutting and chopping, cutting and cutting. Some fierce sewing followed on. She being so fixed-eyed on her work, I slid off, hid myself in my room.

Chapter 3

In that sad room, with the narrow bed, there was one other piece of furniture, a tall old clothes cabinet, lime green painted. When I took off my Ohio jacket, hung it rough on the part-open cabinet door edge…. that cabinet tipped, near fell, due to lacking one foot. A clatter sounded that halted my heart, for down from the top a box fell, a tin one. It's hinged lid burst open on the floorboards. Scattered-out there, dozens of colored barrettes, and two small dolls, one doll a lady in an old-fashioned dress, the other, a man in a uniform of gray. Who, I wondered was the owner of these strange belongings. I placed the contents of the box loose on top of the cabinet, I began a plan. I would hide my few Ohio things in that same tin box. Carefully, I laid in a picture of my mother, a penknife given to me by my father not long before he was to die, an acorn from our garden tree, a nickel, the last money in the world I had. Along with these, lay all the hope I had of getting free. For inside that box would get changed to be Ohio air, from touching Ohio things. It would be a warming feeling to know, that whenever I looked inside that box, smelled the air, I would be home. Soon I hoped, this box and me would be united with our native place.

After some looking around, I found that the drawer at the bottom of that clothes cabinet, if taken out, had space under, a space plenty big to fit a box. There I hid it.

On the narrow bed I lay, a ribbon of pictures shunted past. I saw myself hitch-hiking home, I saw myself in a freight car on the railroad, looking out of a slit, the Ohio county flashing, I saw I was in my old bed, in the old room, safe home…. But the house is empty, the bed gone, the mother gone home to God. If she were alive and here, my mother, what would she tell me to do? She warned me off hitch-hiking, always. "Work Lafe, work for what you want…. the beginning of change is work." The idea came straight as she said it, it came straight on her voice. I made up my mind, tonight I will ask for work.

I was ordered down to dinner; over my chair back, the finished overalls, two pairs. "Underpants and overalls, that's what our men are accustomed with boy, you'd better get accustomed to it…. and no sock wearing neither…. I've clothes washing enough," said Miss Lorraine in an acid voice.

A slab of meat, and black-eyed peas, cooked dead, was the meal before us. After praying grace, there was no talking. Some steady eating went on. I ate but ate little. Mr Snake, his mouth full and spilling said…. "Better food than your Mamma made eh boy?" then brought up a belch that brought a nasty look out of Miss Lorraine. She got up to re-enforce the plates, her back turned, I slid off and away to the room, gripping the two pairs of overalls. I had lost my nerve to ask for work.

The ceiling boards in the bedroom were yellow painted, the paint peeling. I lay staring…. grief came from me as I had never let it out. Tears spilled in torrents down; in waves they emptied, in bouts of hurling grief. An hour or two I had wept gone, the light from the window had died; till grief settled dry, in whimpers, beyond tear making.

Chapter 4

In the morning, eyelids fat from tears, I pulled on the overalls. They hung big off me, were short in leg. I could look down the bib front, clear past my underpants to my knee joints.

"You are at a useless age boy," is what Miss Lorraine said with the point of a knife at breakfast, I had asked for work. "You're too grown for schooling, too young to be any sort of hand about this place." She took a look at the size of her sewing job, said not a thing on that. Snake looked, laughed, his mouth bursting full of food, held in by his hand. "Don't go out in no wind in those boy, you'll end up back in Ohia." If only that could be, I thought. "What's wrong, somebody knuckle your eyes boy?" Meantime Old Kain looked past me, while eating steady. He shifted his looking to me, said, "Ask that old dark roast... Eli.... to give.... you some.... busy work boy." His gassy voice floated over the table. I spoke my bravest.... "Is there any chance of earning some money by working?" There was a horrible quiet. At the end of a pointing fork, Miss Lorraine jabbed.... "Look we ain't rich, not a charity neither, you gets meat, you gets drink, you gets bed, every day; that by itself should be atoned for by a good days work every day." "Give him five cents a day," said Snake in a snide voice, "just so he knows he's not black trash.... on the outside anyway." "Who asked you?".... she shifted the fork his direction. "you'd better give it all the back-effort you've got boy.... five cents plus keep, I'll agree to no more."

I went outside, feeling victory, but doubt. I needed at least 30 dollars for the bus and train home. How many five centses are in 30 dollars? Eli was amongst the grease, wrestling a bolt in an engine part. The part was skidding round on a greasy board. "Grab onto it young boy would you?" For the first time, I had my hands in grease… it felt good. Excited, I told Eli of the plan for five cents a day, and how I intended running off. "They sure is a generous lot them Kains, why at that rate you'll…. let's see, you'll make three hundred sixty-five times five." He worked it out with a bolt in the dirt. "One thousand, eight hundred and twenty-five cents, if you was to work seven days a week, including Christmas and that…. though you better know I don't approve of Sunday or Christmas day working mind." A fortune it sounded, till Eli put it solid to dollars… "Eighteen dollars, twenty-five cents a year! It's a wage that'd make a slave holla SLAVERY!" said Eli. "Do they pay you Eli, are you some sort of a slave?" Eli laughed…. "Next to it boy; they wouldn't pay me if they could get away with it…. Any bosses is like that I guess…. but it ain't much more than a chicken could live off of. We cousins in slavery boy, you and me." He looked at my grief-swollen eyes, looked down.

Eli set me up in the shade, to the left side and below the wood platform where the two young black workers were slow at work sorting metal behind their bins. I had the job of undoing generator motors, get the copper wound middle free. I was glad of some time-using thing to settle my thoughts on, it was still morning, still fresh. Near me, growing, was a small palm tree with the nights damp on it, I wiped off my hands on the ground, began to thumb the leaf, feel the thickness, amazing, like leather, tropical that feel. It was hard to know it was a real living thing. Before coming south, I had only marveled at such things in my picture encyclopedia; yet to these metal sorter boys, it was as everyday as an Ohio bull thistle. One of the metal sorters shouted down…. "Eh boy, that there's a saw palmetto, won't get no bigger than that, watch out for them spiked stems, that's why they calls it 'saw' palmetto, they like saw-hell to walk through. See how it's low growin' padded-out like, with palm cloth, that's a tough race of growin' thing right there boy. I've seen 'em come back after bad fire run across 'em. This whole place must a' been them one time, them and slash pines, 'stead of Junk and Kains."

At the word 'Kains' a shot blasted from in amongst the horizon of cars, a small way off, then another. One of the boys said, "he's at it." After a short space, another shot that ended in spzzzzzing. One boy said to the other in a spoon hand, "Hope that skidding bullet did the job for us." He was nudged quiet by the other. A minute's gap later.... like a hot boar, Snake Kain stormed out from the Palmettos and wrecks, across the clearing, in a line, straight for the metal sorters. They started sorting fast, eyes down. "We goin' to ketch hell now boy, must have missed.... no dead rattler," muttered one to the other. Snake Kain's face was twisted, it was hate, clear and plain. Sweat was on him, gut heaving. I kept low. Snake Kain directed that revolver as if it was a metal finger, pointing first at the platform, then in the air... he yelled, "You black sons of bitches.... I want them bins filled by sundown, or you get your black 'asses out of here and for good." Off he took, leaving dust and silence behind himself. "One day.... OH, one day," said the metal sorter, whose name was Luther, twisting his hands on a piece of iron pipe. They now fell back to their slow action, sorting. Luther leaned my direction, said, "Don't pay no never mind boy, he'll not remember he said it.... he'll be in Pabst Blue Ribbon Beer- can land soon enough." "Recon he's cornered the aluminum market single handed that Snake has," said the other boy.... "go look in back of the house, he has a wood bin, big as this is, it's a mess o' cans, filled high and all spilled."

Eli staggered across the dirt yard, had a box of metal scrap, heaved it up to the two sorters. He took me off to one side, said, "How you doin' boy? Don't get upset over that Snake, he's a twisted boy; been grown twisted that-a-way, like a tree coming up under a mudguard. I've seen him as a tiny thing.... I've seen him as a grown thing. That Old Mr Kain and his wife bent him as he grew; whipped that boy something cruel. Never a hug nor a kind word did he know. I reckon they gave him a Rattlesnake tail as a rattle, you know, when he was a baby…. just so he'd get fixated on something lethal like that. Later times there, they handed down that old Civil War revolver to feed his hate along. After being raised in hate by haters that-a-way, recon he hates his-self more than any other thing or person. After Snake's mother died, Snake hooked Miss Lorraine, married her. Now take Miss Lorraine, there's a woman who uses her tongue same as Snake's old mama did the belt. That Snake boy has no power, and it eats his belly. I recon, the only time I ever do see that Snake boy smile, is when he's holdin' one of them Rattlesnakes, dead. He's proud right then, proud as a slave catcher holdin' a captive… he's nice as sugar right then."

At dinner I got up nerve to ask Snake Kain for my five cents wages. "THE BOSS… of every money thing BOY, is over there, beating on those eggs." Miss Lorraine heard, gave a short sniff, stiffened up her neck. After rattling about in a drawer, she slapped down five cents in front of me on the table board; went back to beating those eggs with an even more ferocious action.

It was a strengthening thing to go back to the room, to my secret Ohio box, put my first wages coin in, to know it was my first step out of this Hell place.

Chapter 5

On Sunday, I was woken at 6 a.m. to a vicious knocking.... then, "Get Decent." By this I understood I was to put on my Ohio outfit for church. How strange-feeling and close it all fit, after the overalls: the pants, the jacket, the shirt, all at once, too small. Could I have grown that much in a week? The socks had the effect of boiling me.

Into the pick-up truck Miss Lorraine, Snake Kain, Old Kain and myself compacted. I cooked more, squashed up against Mr Snake, whose suit was in distress, whose shirt was in distress more, to the button shedding stage. There was that smell of rot I knew, not hidden even by massive after-shave. Snake Kain's hair was licked flat with grease over his balding place into a dog tail at the back, shiny, but not from shampoo work. Miss Lorraine wore a hat, stabbed through by hat pins.

With Old Kain driving, fitted in just that way, we took off out from there. Past endless wrecks, that ended, past wood houses needing paint, past porches with tub-and-wringer washing machines, past porches with old sofas on, past Winn Dixie grocery store, to a wood church with a steeple going up of wood; painted hard white, like a bride-dress placed on the land. And the faces of those going in were white. We stood inside, we kneeled, we sat, we stood, we sang. The singing was of people with strong lungs, but mournful it was, a sad but strong feel to it, like those not yet quite broken. It looked to me the most fixated prayer-maker ever was 'longside of me in the pew, her neck jutted forward, her lip's making prayers.

There she was, Miss Lorraine Kain, she attended strong to listening; a sermon that rose furious, then not. It caused me to find other occupying things in the lulls. I counted hats, took up fidgeting the prayer book to a spin in my hands, which stopped right fast, as a slap from Miss Lorraine came down. I dropped the book, picked it up, saw that Mr Snake was the only one without a book. I handed it to him. Miss Lorraine bent her head, pinch lipped whispered…. "You stupid boy…. keep tha' book….use it…. Snake can't read." I was amazed at that fact, amazed at being called stupid in the face of that.

Before we came out from there, we had to wake-up Old Mr Kain, who was making noises not of this earth, out of his neck.

The way back was…. Old Kain driving, making strange sounds, swerves, unsteady moves. He turned on the radio to keep his eyelids up. The song 'I Will Survive' ripped into that hot space from the black radio station. "Turn that black trash off," yelled Snake…. "Hey Pa, hear about the execution Friday morning?…. they got 'Old Sparkey' working again after 15 years." "'Bout time," said Old Kain. "Yep Pa, must be a fair old log jam of them murderers waiting on that old electric chair. That guy Spenkelink, he's only the first. Hope they clear a few of them Midnights out next…. Guess they had to kill a white man first, wouldn't you say Pa? Stop the big 'D' word comin' up."…. "How about discrimination…. discrimination again' the white race?" said Old Kain, as he swerved sudden into the driveway. I was glad to get out of that sweat-box, and out of my Ohio outfit, which like me was cooked damp.

Chapter 6

It was not long after the big rains came, late June, I had been here one month. Nights came in even hotter now and made for poor sleep. At first light, I sat out on the steps of the metal-sorting platform, shifted my sight across the acres of car roofs painted dull with dew. Off to the right, there was one lone tree, a massive live oak, 'Old as Indians' Eli had said when he told me the many things about it. Its fat arms stretched massive out, the top-side of each arm, bristled thick with air plants as if hair. From every branch and high-up twig, Spanish moss hung ragged off it, like something mournful. White egrets, newly awake, perched before the waking sky. Beyond the oak, the metal sun disc came slow, powering up the east, big and copper and humming, through a milk haze. It fired up the world of the tree in gold, as it stained the broken world below. Such a calm came through me then, it seemed the day was blessed.

It wasn't too long after that the human world joined the day. I was soon undoing metal from metal at my usual shaded spot. Luther and Nathan, the two metal sorters, stood behind their bins, were slow at sorting, and Eli bent over the chest of another wreck. It was then that this day became like no other. A white limousine drove in, moved past us workers like a thing floating. It pulled to a stop across the dirt clearing and in front of the Kain's wood house. The metal sorters stopped sorting, Eli lifted his head, we all looked that direction.

There were suitcases lifted out; there was a small figure with a flash of electric blue and white cotton cloth; there was Miss Lorraine and Old Kain as a greeting party; there was Snake hovering at back, trying to be that too. They went in with the new arrival, leaving Snake to haul the suitcases. As the limousine floated out, it passed like a spirit thing, like the soul of one of these old wrecks floating out.

The sun had only got up the sky a small way more, when the figure in the white cotton dress and electric blue waist-sash came skipping out from that neglected house across the dirt and dust to in front of our work place. It was as if some blended extra thing was with the morning air, like menthol or lemon; for she was perfect made. "Why Miss Roxella, you're home," said Eli across to her. She didn't answer, turned her foot in the dirt, spun herself, then off she tripped like a blown petal leaf, back toward the house and gone.

"Who is that girl?" I said to Eli. "Why, that there is Snake and Miss Lorraine's daughter of course boy…. You didn't know they had a daughter? That's young Miss Roxella Kain." I was glad to share sandwiches with Eli at lunch. The sight of the unknown girl had given me the jitters, I didn't want to go in. "Young Miss Roxella,"… said Eli, between chewing, "is sent off to private high school in Mississippi… same school as her mother was at. Miss Lorraine herself had something of that same spirit about her once, when she come here a dozen years past. With these years of influences on her, she be what she is now. How that Snake captured such a lady of high blood back then, still to this day is a puzzlement. She come here a lady, with lady speech, lady wrappings, but the years have sure seen that fade off her. Miss Lorraine is one of two sisters, the Butcher Sisters of Tupelo Mississippi. The other sister, a woman of high breedin' equal still to what Miss Lorraine once was, came here one time, lodged but one night, never was seen here again. Young Miss Roxella stays with that sister, is coached up by that sister, is schooled by the finest."

"But Eli, how could such a beautiful creature as Miss Roxella come out of two such ugly makers?" "Why, boy, she came from an orphanage, 'bout twelve year back, when she was a little'n going on three… adopted she is. When the doctor told Miss Lorraine, she was barren ground there, she got set on adoptin' a little'n… had to be a girl, so she could mould her to her liking, and mould her she did, without a hug or kiss. Miss Lorraine swore she would never raise a daughter in what she called, 'This rust heap', but that's just what happened. She blames Mr Snake, I know she does for bringing her to this."

I had a crisis of nerves that didn't rest; at the dinner table, Snake and Young Miss Roxella were at one side, me to the other, Miss Lorraine and Old Kain at their usual head and tail places. I had a job to know where to put my sight, I looked at the plate. They never introduced me to this white-faced girl, except to say, 'this is the boy that occupies your old room Roxella.' Some brittle silence followed, punctured only by the clicking of Old Kain's false teeth. Old Kain now stretched his neck up, which showed off his neck flap very well. Catching breath, he started in on a schoolboy feat of memory sharpness by parroting off all the president's names, from George Washington backwards down the years, till after many gaps for breath he got to where Mr. Lincoln should have been, and put in Confederate President Jefferson Davis. This brought cheers and hand clapping out of his listeners, who must have heard this same performance a bunch of times, Snake yelling, "Looks like Old Abe got voted out of existin' there Pa!" But I kept my sweating hands flat on my upper legs under the table. "Grandpap," said Miss Roxella, "your memory is unclouded as ever". This triggered the old man off into more belching talk…. "Back in better…. days then, if I was to…. walk down the…. sidewalk say…. down town Fort Myers and…. a n****r was…. coming at me…. on the same side…. why naturally…. he would cross…. the road…. walk to the other…. side, to give…. free path for…. the white man…. that was the time…. when black and white…. both knew…. where they was at…. like Crows and

Swans.... now they think.... they own the sidewalk.... them black Crows do."

Now Young Miss Roxella spoke, her voice pure, sharp as a fresh cut lemon. "Not everything has changed dear Grandpap.... separation of races is with us still, only now it's voluntary separatin'. In the middle school I was at here, before I was sent off to more civilized surroundin's I learned more than chemistry, I learned black engine oil and white milk don't mix. Stir them up as you like, they will always separate out. Seems to me there are four sorts of girls, poor black girls they know their kind, poor white girls, they stick to their kind, there are moneyed white girls, the same, but the very few moneyed black girls, and the mixed-race ones.... they don't know what they were made as." "Serves 'em right," said Snake, they're black all the way through.... proves the theory don't it.... they ain't fit for money nor white blood." "Well," said Young Miss Roxella, "I do thank providence that I am now in a school with girls from some of the finer families, where the only black face to be seen is shining a toilet bowl."

I was finding it a job to get the glass of water to my mouth, my hand in such a shake. I had my head up, managing to drink, when Young Miss Roxella fired up her eyes at me. My glass overfilled my mouth to both sides, down my windpipe went the water... bursting me into a splutter. It now looked just as if I had wet my overall pants. All shaken, I got up bent, ran to the stairs. Miss Lorraine jagged after me "You'll wear 'em till they dry boy!" Snake laughed me all the way up.

I sat on the bed-edge, thought of Young Miss Roxella, what must she think of me now? How much better she might have found me, if I had been in good clothes. But like a cut lemon, its insides shown to the air, Young Miss Roxella Kain had already lost some of her freshness when she opened her mouth.

Chapter 7

In the days that followed on, Young Miss Roxella showed herself to have a love of collecting and pressing flowers of every color. This lone occupying thing she took up, for she had shed away any friends she had had from former school days close by. At every chance, in a beautiful white dress, she would go, swinging a flower press in a careless hold in amongst the field of wrecks. Young Miss Roxella had a way of making a walk in that church day dress, done to get our eyes chasing her. Every morning she walked past us workers with a high neck, a forward chin, playing with one bit of her hair. Some days, the wind would press her, describing out her legs and body. Some days the breeze would play her dress like a tune. Past she would go, on purpose slow, on purpose not looking, for she always glanced back after to catch our eyes on her. I had hope, more than any hope, that that glance was for me. The metal sorters up behind their bins would nudge, say, 'Nice lumps,' make eyes back and laugh, till Snake Kain one day saw, gave brutal threats their way. On future days they would lower their heads, only their eyes looking up, whenever Young Miss Roxella flagged past.

With Luther the metal sorter gone for the week, I now stood under the sun, behind a metal sorting bin. For that week I was to be a proper metal sorter. Nathan was to my left, behind his bin, stripped to the waist, blue black under the forcing sun. Nathan said, "Hey boy, that up there is what the

Mexicans call the 'Eye of God', sure feels more like the 'Eye of the Devil' right now don' it?" The mounded tray of mixed scrap to be sorted had been laid out since early, and was so hot, when I picked up a piece of greasy cast aluminum, I was in a hurry to drop it. Nathan laughed, "Na boy, you'll last but five minutes without gloves," he threw across a pair of oiled-up ones. Soon even with these, heat got through. "Plenty sweat, not much money on this game, boy," said Nathan…. "Only green we likely to see is corrosion green on this 'ere brass!" Red brass, yellow brass, copper in his bin, cast aluminum in mine. That's how the sorting went, with me asking, "What's this part from?"

Most of that long day through the sun threw acid at us, till he showed his mercy late, by loading the shadow of the parts shed on us. By then, my face was blood swollen, blood at my ears pumping, when a woozy thing came on me; I staggered back. Nathan poured a bottle of water over my head. "Set back against the building boy, drink yourself up to the bloated pig stage, and rest-up…. you'll toughen up boy. Tomorrow, get bloated to start with, drink often, you'll last better, 'till you gets tempered hard to the sun." I had new respect for the work of these metal sorters. What looked like nothing of a job to the stander and looker, took great hidden toughness. At dinner I ate not much, for I was water swollen still, but with a thirst that would not be put down. Young Miss Roxella stared to her food plate with not a look for me. My fever for her should have gone quiet, like a fever starved, but it burned hotter than any sun ever did.

In the narrow room, I sat on the mattress end, travelled my sight across broken paint, wood cracks on the inside of the shut door. I felt no sadness like before, Young Miss Roxella had fixed herself inside my eyes, like a light bulb long stared at. Where Ohio had been, she now was; where a solid plan of escape had been, she now was. Her face had thieved Ohio out of me right now.

If only I too had been brought up in hate, she would like me then, I know it. I shrunk the thought, yet it clung at me. The only black men I had ever known were Eli and the metal sorters. Could I hate these men for her? It was a thought against all my Ohio bringing-up days, yet her cold white face haunted, smiling approvin'. I slept disturbed.

Every inch of my working day and into my sleep, thoughts of that magical girl ruled my brain, but, two days had to pass, before I could get her to notice me. We had just lifted our eyes from making the grace prayer, the dinner laid…. Snake said, "Hope you're not getting too friendly with them black slackers out there…. the black don't rub off, but the slackery sure do." He wiped the heat off the back of his neck with a napkin. I heard the words come out of me…. "You don't need to worry about that, I'm not a slacker, I'm not a n****r lover neither…. I don't like n****rs any more than you do." The words came out natural sounding. Young Miss Roxella Kain fired up a glance, a triumph look, the wisp of a smile. My blood fizzed, my brain turned red. Snake took on a look of someone meeting confusion. He jumped his looking from the black-eyed peas on his plate, to my blue eyes and back, then settled on the peas. He shifted those peas about slow with his fork, said "Any white boy who uses the 'N' word, better mean it." He stared…. looking him right back, I said, "Yes Sir, I do mean it." He looked right satisfied as Miss Roxella's eyes took a sparkle. "Why this is a fair turnabout boy," said Snake…. "we'll soon have a real Southern Kain salvaged out from that northern wreck," and went on chasing his black-eyed peas. My belly was in a mix-up, as I left the table still red faced.

The guilt I felt over what I had said, stung me, especially when I was with Eli. Whenever I was in the sight of Young Miss Roxella, though, something else took over.

Chapter 8

"I draft you boy." I knew the voice. I stopped, one foot down on the front porch steps. "I draft you boy," Snake again said. He was sitting balanced back on a porch wicker chair, a thick brown leather belt holding in his overall gut, boot heels rested up on the rail. "I draft you boy to be my second set of eyes and ears." There was sly in his eyes. "There could be fattened-up wages in it boy…. you being one of us and all. Miss Lorraine's VERY protectin' of her only daughter…. understand me boy?" The wicker chair arm made a crack. "Being as I'm busy afternoons, I need eyes and ears out there in the work area, you think on it boy." I nodded his direction, went on down the porch steps.

To be his snooping tool, how could I do that, how could I live with that after? It was a way of getting her to like me though, being on her father's good side. But if she ever found out my informing was to do with her…. would she ever care for me ever? I didn't have much time to churn this. Late morning Snake Kain called me down to just inside the parts shed door. "Well boy, wha' you have to tell me 'bout that black scum out here?" his voice too loud for Nathan up on the sorting platform not to hear. I moved further in, letting the door slam behind. I whispered, "Nothing to report yet."

"Com' on boy, what they bin up to talking about?"

"They just said Young Miss Roxella hasn't been out lately."

"That's ALL they said? …. swear it boy"

"Yes."

"You keep your nose down and your ears up boy, I'll be expectin' reports daily."

When I stood again, back at the sorting bin, terror was in me. Did Nathan hear? Nathan would look my way, sniff, look my way again. The only sound was metal parts being dropped in bins. As the afternoon rotted past, I knew for sure he had heard…. there was nothing to be said.

"That boy's comin' along a treat mother," said Snake Kain, as he blew his nose on his napkin…. "Got them midnights out there working a fine lick." Roxella lifted her beautiful head, her eyes burned up at me. "I think we should up his wages some mother,"…. he picked his teeth, "fifty cents a day." "I'll be the decider of that!" Miss Lorraine chopped in…. "Let him prove hi'self." I had better wages already, in the burning look that came out of Young Miss Roxella Kain. Next lunchtime Snake Kain fired more questions my way. The only thing I could blurt was, "They say you're drunk afternoons." "Drunk, my arse." And he breathed a laugh that stank.

Chapter 9

Next day, neither Snake nor Roxella were at breakfast. I ate down the bacon, managed the grits…. it was that or starve. As I went out onto the front porch, I passed the sprawling legs of Snake Kain. He sat in a wicker chair that was unravelling at it's legs, he was cleaning the revolver. "Know what this here is boy?" he said in a voice not too bad. He spat on the barrel, rubbed it on his overall leg…. "This here's a Colt .44 caliber 1860 Civil War revolver…. This here has been passed hand to hand down the years of Southern Kains. This piece fought for the Confederacy boy, it belonged in the hand of my great, great grandfather Wade Kain, and he was brother to your great, great grandfather, Olin Kain, who we are ashamed to whisper fought for the Yankees…. Follow me boy? Didn't know you had Bluebelly killers and n****r haters so close on your blood did you boy?"….. It passed through me…. I did know that. "This piece has killed both Yankee snakes and rattlesnakes, boy." As he was tending to point the revolver my direction, I was quick away.

The sun that morning was coming like a stove, as I walked out. Over by the metal sorter's platform, there was a new sight, a rust-pitted truck, parked to one side. On it were piled, four, could be five wrecked cars, I went closer. Down from the cab got a big built tall white man, with fairish hair. "Hey," he greeted Nathan the metal sorter, by slapping his hand that he reached down from the platform…. "How's Clay then?" said Nathan. "I'd feel better out of this gaddam sun," said Clay, who then greeted Eli with a slap on the back. "I'm having trouble with the old truck Eli…. thought I might not make it back here," said Clay. He opened the hood, steam or smoke rose up out from the engine place. I started my work on the platform next to the silent Nathan.... all till lunch Clay was disappeared, bent in that engine, un-bolting, and bolting. After ages, he said, "Let's crank her up." In a mess of sound and smoke that old truck burst to life like a dead man woken. As Clay wiped his hands off, he gave a satisfied look. The sun had moved, laid down a shadow over one side of that truck. He greeted me with a smile did Clay. Eli said, "Come on boy, share my lunch if you like." We sat our backs against the truck wheel, Eli, Clay and me in a line. "Not bologna again!" said Clay, as he lifted open a sandwich edge. "Why does she always give me Bologna?"

He peeled it out from the bread with dirty fingers, flung it, a soft wet spinning thing onto a near wrecked car's hood. It started to sweat, to curl, to cook... "Mmmmmm, smells good don't it?" said Clay with a laugh.... "Yeh boy, God's headlamp sure working overtime today," said Eli as he handed me a tuna fish sandwich. I liked it, but it chewed a bit warm as I worked into it. "Two of these wrecks I just brought had deaths in 'em," said Clay. The Chevy up there is a mess inside, wouldn't be a bad idea Eli to give her a hosing out." I stopped short on the tuna fish, hid what was left in back of me.

"So you're the Northern Kain boy," said Clay.... "How'd you like life with the Southern Kains eh boy? Not what you was used to I'll bet.... Most whites round her are not so much like them Kains these days, not no more anyway boy. The Kains is an extreme race; though I will say there's quite a few lesser Kains about as I've run into.... Anyhow boy you'll soon get used to this twisted place.... reckon when you've growed a good few more inches boy, you'll be telling us all what to do!"

"This boy don't intend stayin'," said Eli, wiping crumbs off his lips. "Well if I was a boy, I'd stick at it here, wouldn't find me turning my back on half this land... must be worth a good fair bit I'd say." I looked at Clay blank. "They didn't tell you? .... they didn't, did they? .... You're half owner of this fine establishment boy." "Well I'll be jiggered…. You're not joking are you Clay," said Eli…. amazed, almost to the place of being more amazed than I was. "How do you know that?" asked Eli "Snake his-self told me. One night there, we got to drinking, he forgot his tongue I guess, let it out, the whole story come out like a glob…. 'bout your father up north there, putting in half the money thirty five year back, and being half owner, to get the Kains started in business here. When your Papa died, it went to your Ma, and now to you boy. Snake told me you was expected any day, by bus or train…. and here you are. Guess Miss Lorraine and Snake had to take you in, you being blood an' all and owning half of what they think is theirs. I do reckon though boy, its a bad sign, they never told you you owned half…. I do know they've been trying to separate themselves from your family for years. Didn't your Momma nor your Poppa never tell you you owned it boy?" "No, they would talk of the southern Kains from time to time, but they never did say a thing on owning anything. After my mother was buried, the house was sold to pay off the bank and all the other debts. I was handed a train ticket, an address, put on a train out of Ohio by a welfare person, I had nobody left there." "Look boy, don't let Snake know I told you this, he's vicious bad when he's gets roiled up." "I won't tell any of them Mr Clay… but you are certain it's true?" "Certain as Snake's words boy…. you watch them Kains, they really is like rattlesnakes…. watch they don't bite you, or worse, turn you into a snake." I had to let this new fact sink in. I watched Clay unload the terrible cargo with a crane, I watched him back his empty truck under the raised platform, till one of the sorting bins was above. Nathan pulled a long pin, two doors fell open, all the insides of the bin emptied avalanche sounding onto the truck. Clay now headed toward the house, he disappeared for a good long time, returned, jumped up on the platform, had quiet words with Nathan. As he climbed into the cab of his old truck, he threw a puzzled eye my direction. I watched this bringer of strange news drive off.

At evening I lay awake. My mind went back to the first

night when I overheard that gassy voice, which was Old Mr Kain's, also Miss Loraine saying, 'We'll get free of him soon enough, let some time pass,' it fitted with what Clay had told me. So that's what they are after…. separating this land and business from my family…. and I alone am my family. I wasn't sure if I really didn't want to get cheated out of such a prize after all.

A few more days rusted past before Clay was again arriving with another mangled cargo. As a big shadow edged across the sorting platform, the sun west falling, with Nathan and the newly returned Luther gone for the day, Clay sat himself up on the platform, legs off the edge. He started to roll a cigarette, slow, with an angled look my direction, said, "What I'm hearin' from Snake I don't believe boy…. You turning into a core Southern Kain…. What greased that?" The red in my face was reply enough. Clay still rolling his cigarette said, "I dated a nurse once, psychiatric ward nurse, worked out at Charter Glades Mental Hospital, good looker, built well, nice headlamps… that's beside the point…. Anyhow she told me about all these experiments done on monkeys, back in the fifties there. Bet you're thinking 'what's that got to do with anything,' well boy lots. Those monkeys were taken from their mothers at an early age, put in cages with wire mothers called 'Iron Maidens'…. they got no comfort poor little mites, they were cold hard metal mothers, they only got milk. To cut a long thing short, these baby monkeys got terrible messed-up…. couldn't relate to no other monkeys, couldn't do all the normal things monkeys do, like holdin' each other and that. Once they'd passed a certain age there, the damage was permanent. I've known the Kain family too many years now, I've seen Young Miss Roxella from the day she was brought here, an adopted child. Don't expect much of that young lady boy, and she is a lady, but a lady with deep deep problems under that beautiful surface, problems bred into her by her 'Iron Maiden' of a mother Miss Lorraine. Snake's old mama was an 'Iron Maiden' too of sorts… cold as they come… hard as wire… not a loving sinew in her, he had a childhood built on punishment, it's a wonder he didn't turn out even worse. When Snake was practically just out of diapers there, went for an older woman, another 'Iron Maiden' shape of Miss Lorraine, to rule him with a loveless fist, that same fist that now shapes Roxella. Believe me boy some girls are so perfect, hard to believe they ever go shit, but behind that showroom window, there's a person. Don't expect anything of that ice princess, she's damaged goods, a child created to crave love but never to give it, never to accept it neither…. a real man breaker. If there's any small bit of sap to be risen in that female, a man firm on his beliefs is the only chance. So boy, I hope you drop this n****r hating nonsense before you really start to believe it." Clay finished rolling his cigarette, went back to his truck, it sat heavy with scrap. I watched him out, as he took the bend that truck rose and sank. A heavier load was sinking in me.

Nathan, being the more wordy of the two metal sorters, wasn't able to keep the wall of quiet for more than two days; maybe Clay had told him the real reason for my turn of face, or maybe his love of talk was just too strong, whichever, the horrible silence ended. The newness of sorting metal was off me, I was glad Luther had returned and I was back in my old job, in the shade, also by now Snake had worn tired of my empty reports.

Chapter 10

On Friday night, early, we sat to a meal of cold sausages. Miss Lorraine was wearing her Sunday things; pronounced grace before us, ate but one sausage, pulled her gloves on, skewered her hat on, slapped five cents on the table plank and with Old Mr Kain and Roxella, walked fast out.

The silence was bad, Snake and me sitting, till he broke it. "Friday night is Greyhound night at the Naples, Fort Myers greyhound track…. See y'all there." Snake Kain said it in a bad 'radio voice' …. "Gone dog betting that's what – left us with chores…. 'OR ELSE.' She likes them dishes washed a certain fashion boy, does Miss Lorraine…. put in exact places…. you take the garbage out…. if I don't do the gadam dishes just right we'll both ketch hell." After the dish banging fell silent, he put himself on Old Kain's chair, with a six-pack of Blue Ribbon beer before him. Knees spread, arms spread, gripping the table edge, he looked a fat copy of his father, and the sudden owner of all. His face went mild…. "I'm still worried you getting too thick again with them blacks out there boy…. look to your heritage." "My heritage?" I said, nervous. "Remember do you? what I said 'bout having southern n****r haters so close to your blood, well your Northern Kains wasn't exactly great n****r lovers neither. Y' see boy, your Great Great Grandfather Olin Kain, and my Great Great Grandfather Wade Kain grew as brothers there in Atlanta Georgia… when thirteen, Olin Kain ran off, ended up up north in Ohia. They still kept the odd letter between 'em those two brothers. When the big fight come, few years on, your ancestor Olin, sorry to say, joined the Bluebelly cavalry in Ohia. Wade, true to his foundations, joined the Confederate infantry at Atlanta, under John Bell Hood. Wade ended up being taken captive by Sherman's men, at Ezra church Georgia, got shipped north to a prison camp at Elmira, N.Y. Your northern Bluebelly ancestor Olin traced Wade there, wrote him. They didn't hold Wade long before he got free, got south to fight again for the Confederacy. Why for all we know them two brothers might have fought each other boy. This letter must 'a been in Wade's pocket through many a fat and lean time I should bet. This letter's bin read to me a bunch of times." He skidded the letter across the boards.... "Read.... read."

September 5th eighteen and sixty four

Brother,

Hope you are not too low at being taken captured by our forces at Ezra Church. A better fate than so many.... Between being free and being dead, you are in the purgatory place, and might have got-off lucky. I hear you have a small wound. You won't be glad to hear, the Union Army press the Rebs. Constantly.

We will set free the darkies, if it takes grabbing every black toe to do it. I have had sights of a black regiment on yesterday. They make a fair line-up, like a row of burnt fence posts.

Our mother wrote me of your plight. I hope this letter reaches you. I hope there is food enough.

Your brother in blue cloth,

Olin Kain

"Well what do you think on that boy? Not exactly a complimenter of the black race is he, that Great Great Grandpa o' yours? Remember boy, we Kains goes proud way back and that's Southern back. Our past is Southern past and Kains should stick true in our beliefs; our beliefs should be your beliefs, if you is a true Kain. Keep them blacks where they know their place… think hard on it boy."

A bitter fizz just nearly burst my nose, Snake let out a gut laugh. "Never tried beer have you boy, looks like that beer don't like you much…. have another swig, let's see what sort of belly you've got." My next swallow was about as fierce, burning bubbles lifted my brain.

We now sat on the porch stairs, out front of that old wood house and stared out. The moon was fat, full faced over the wrecks before us, all in weird light. "Com'on boy, you're not drinkin'!" I took more swallows. "See over there, see it boy, the Buick, the one set on its own there, not far from the sortin' bins. That there's a 1936 Buick…. it's all stove in at the right side front, see that. You might think we see all cars as things to scavenge boy, but that there's special that automobile, intact, just as it was set there before I was born. Old Mr Kain, my Papa keeps that as a sort of monument piece… back then, round 1937 that was owned by a family. The children was sisters, good lookers I'm told, blonde, good teeth and all, teenagers they was. One night, those two sisters drivin' back from a picture show, stopped for root beer…. didn't lock no cars nor nothin' them days. When they took off from there, they had another passenger, most likely hid flat on the floor of the back… a black name of Willie Stark. This Willie Stark tied and raped them girls in that car, threw 'em out at the highway side. They was found like that, dead with their throats slit. When news got off, there was the biggest man search seen here, dogs and everything out. That Willie Stark was chased by every man and his brother-in-law. He was spotted in that same Buick headed north on a back road, chased till he took a curve bad, ended up against a cabbage palm.

Soon there was cars stopped all about, nobody wanted to get too close in. One man fired some shots into the driver's side door, they dragged that boy out wounded. No law had arrived, so they carried that n****r squirming to a barn, strung him up: when he was seen next day, nobody said nothin', the police called it suicide. That black son-of-a-bitch had good justice done him right then on the spot. You should go, go look it over, that Buick in the day boy, them bullet holes is still in the door. It's a fine old piece that automobile, its old license plate and all still on it. It's from a time when the world had things straight."

By now my head had left dry ground. I got up to go to the toilet, could hardly keep standing. "I thin' I'd better go in"…. Snake gave an evil laugh as I had trouble getting the screen door. Inside I made for the stairs. It was as if I was on a ship, a first-time sailing-man, I was heaved this way, and then the floor came rushing, then fell away.

In the bed it was good to be on some still thing a second, till the room hurtled itself in circular fashion round. I tried to catch up with my eyes…. those yellow walls were flat out spinning.

That's the last I knew, till morning time, when the pain of a drink headache got to be a known thing.

Chapter 11

It happened on the Friday, during our morning break. Old Mr Kain came across the dirt yard, slow toward us workers as we sat. Luther said low, nudging, "Look out… look what's comin'." "Eli"…. said Old Kain, loud as he could manage…. "Eli," and he hooked his finger. Eli was already to his feet and soon limping there, holding his sandwich behind his overall leg. "Eli…. I want you to…. clear out some of…. that trash and weeds…. round the old…. Buick there…. and see to maintainin' it…. in a better state." "Yes Sir, Mr Kain Sir, I'll see to it right off." Eli was touching his forehead with his free hand, giving small bows. Eli could not sit, could not finish his sandwich, this burden of work left him unsettled. When Old Kain was out of ear reach, Luther said…. "Eli, I have respect for your age, but that was plain-out sickenin', you the backwardest old man I ever came across. Why you always bow to that dried-up old son of a bitch slave overseer?" "Habit, I guess…. habit"…. said Eli looking to the direction of Old Kain. "Him and me go back plenty years." "Well," said Luther, "What fit then don't fit now." "Like a nervous tick I got I guess from the old time," said Eli. "Looked more deep to me, more like a nervous chigger, something deep in your skin old man." Luther did not smile.

Eli was soon swiping at the dried grass and palmettos with a tool, the type of which I had never seen. Like a big stirrup, angled, on a longish handle, a flat cutting blade, sharp to both edges at the bottom, and that blade cut on both swings of it. Holding the wood handle, Eli swung side to side in a rhythm, singing…. "I'll Riiiii….. ze again' yes I'll riiii…… ze again, death won't keep me in the ground." "Snake Kain told me about this old Buick Eli," I said as I stood and watched his work, "and about the bullet holes in the door." "Yeh boy, there they still is." He smoothed his old black fingers over the dead paint, "A bit rusted round, but there they is. There was talk that Willie Stark didn't do it, was some white guy," said Eli, "And that it was found out but kept quiet. There was talk that Willie Stark found this car by the roadside, keys in it; that he did the crime of car stealin' but not of rape and murder. Even if the truth come out, it wouldn't have done poor Willie Stark no good anyhow, he was already a dead n****r on the end of a rope and finished before he started." Eli kept on humming and cutting in time.

Close onto lunch rain came on. Clay arrived with another load of dead cars, he yelled for Eli and me to climb up in his rusty cab in the dry, we ate lunch there, Eli sharing his. As rain dribbled down the windshield front, a damp bleakness came on us. Eli said, "They just tore me off a strip, those two black boys did for showing respect to that Old Mr Kain." "Well," said Clay, "Guess it drills a tooth in 'em to see it Eli. They ought to get mean at that Old Kain instead, but they're scared of him see, it's deep, deep in 'em even if they don't know it. Old Kain's mind is same as elastic, gone perished round the year 1860. I think his son Snake, he's made of the same perished stuff, him goin' round with that Civil War firearm and all. I guess for Snake, coming up in such a Confederate fixated family, then being shipped off to South Vietnam…. got shipped out there just three years after he married Miss Lorraine, 19 he was. Guess two defeats is too much for Old Snake, Civil War and Vietnam."

"Snake in Vietnam?" I said, Clay nodded, chewing, dragged up his shirt sleeve, showed a sunk-in place on his arm. "Drafted, him and me both, some Gook with an AK47 made that…. nearly lost my arm. If that'd been say, a lead minie ball from Civil War time, I'd likely have to drive this truck one handed; or a wagon them days…. They'd have taken my arm off for sure, make no mistake, that was a civil war too, that Vietnam hell, a north trying to tell a south how to live. That's what civil wars is, family flights, and the worst of flights boy…. the worst of all fights to get in the middle of. When we was shipped home, nobody wanted to know us. Everybody wants to forget a loser. Makes you think don't it, wonder how them defeated Southern boys felt after the Civil War ended, and how they was treated by their own kind."

"Well boy," said Eli, "Guess you must know, I look at the Civil War different. A struggle to get us unchained, yes… either way it fell out though, there was plenty of bad to go round for the black race. Black people was at a lose, lose place in time there. If the South had won, or made peace, and slavery was left as it was, who can say what might have been. Guess I'd be workin' for nothing now, 'stead of next to nothin'. Change is pitiful slow boy, for some blacks I hear about, it's improvin' but after 100 years or so, full freedom hasn't quite trickled down this far I guess."

With these heavy thoughts, our eating ended. I slipped down from the cab of Clay's truck, and walked in the lightly settling rain to the border of the sea of wrecks. The puddles were all floated with oil rainbow colors. I looked at the endless sight of car roofs shining, reds and yellows came vivid out in that wet. It was a sight more haunted-sad than any graveyard looked at, for here was the smell and sound of breaks, the sound of crash noise fixed; raw terrible last moment screams stopped, in jagged metal and wires all sticking out.

A mournful carcass lay close near me, that I know there was death in, a gray Chevrolet, mangled in flat at the front, it lay part in weeds, part on dirt. All under one edge of it the silver rain dribbled off; it carried rust down like blood, to stain the dirt in dark to light-brown little puddle circles. I saw there a Carolina wren gripping onto the window-edge of this frozen metal nightmare. She had twigs in her beak, she danced on her legs, she bobbed, and with clear eye, looked at me steady, till skipping the air, she flew inside the car, to where she was building a nest in the glove compartment.

A little after, Eli came over, put his hand on my shoulder, said "Yeh boy, it sure is a sad-makin' sight, especially in wet…… not all are wrecks of crashes though boy; I'd say a good lot of 'em just plain wore out. Those have a softer end to their history. Whichever way boy, those wrecks is haunted…. haunted by death or by life."

That night, my thoughts spread out into dark, through bedroom walls, to all the nightmares, to all the frozen screams and souls and ghosts that were out there round that old house on all sides. As my ears searched every tick of wood in the cooling house, each tick gave a startle. I stayed that way till day, till the sun rescued me out of it.

Chapter 12

I passed through the morning of Monday, having as little to do with the Kains as I could. Eli told me I was too clean of a worker, "Boy," he said… "If you don't get no grease on them there overalls soon, Miss Lorraine will brand you a dead weight on this business…. I'll give you a tip boy, smear a bit of axel grease here, some there, see, as a sort of make-up job, that'll give you a better look."

At lunch time, Snake Kain, Old Kain and myself, filed into the kitchen for eating, and sat. She took a bothered look at us did Miss Lorraine, as if a set of pigs had settled at her kitchen table; Snake Kain made vocals as if a true pig, that had just heard the clatter of a bucket handle. I looked around but there was no Roxella.

Fried up slops is what we got…. as if breakfast, lunch and dinner had been forced and worried into patties. She skidded a plate to each nuisance, said grace with a face of …. 'what we about to receive…. is a slap round the ear.' Snake said across to me, "Watch that n****r Eli he'll spoil a white boys brain, turn it black." Meantime Miss Lorraine went back to taking out her botheration, by hitting the chair legs as she broomed round our feet….I was quick out of there.

Near to five o'clock that day, as shadows spilled long, I started to dread another meal…. Eli, feeling my dread, threw an orange my way, said, "Let's take a stride about this place boy."

We took a path that skirted the edge of the Kain land; that took us to the far edge of the land, the Kain's old house looked small, and I was happy for it. "Now here's a bunch of automobiles," said Eli…. "Here's a bunch of wrecks that I do believe the Kain family has forgotten exist…. they's mostly 1940's and 50's models. Some of these here long wide wrecks would be classics now, if they had any guts left. Look at them fins on that Cadillac…. don't see fins like that these days, why, you could fly straight up to Heaven on those boy!" He rubbed the old paint with his worn old hand, as if rubbing off time.

"See that rusted line, rustin' across, the same level on all; 'bout a third way up the doors there, see it? That's from the time of hurricane, back in 1960. Saw it pass through here out of a pair of younger eyes, had no radio them days, normal work day, black sky, windy, Kains never said nothing about hurricane. I was bent inside that Oldsmobile engine, 'bout where you're at now boy, felt water in my left boot, worn through soles them days…. fierce wind got up, sky scowled, took shelter, things got worse. I was quick reminded how close the ocean was, water swilled in fast, water come up cold, to the depth of a man's overall crotch; water swelled like the ocean swells. I was caught out in it boy, trying to wade back to safety. Rain came on sudden, blowed fierce in across the water's face; rain blowed flat in like lead bullets. Each wreck was turned to be a Noah's Ark of sorts; snakes, cockroaches, ants, lizards, rats all climbed up the wrecks, inside and out; every make of creature life was there together above that swell; every color of enemy and friend, all made level by fear, as it is with mankind in war and disaster time; all made houseless by water, all gripped to life by their small legs, by their bodies, by their claws, by even their teeth; as squalls pushed in and dragged some off to death…. As I waded out, I saw floating railroad ties carrying strange crews, I saw snakes gripped round steering wheels, I saw a rattlesnake occupying the back seat of a fiiiine looking wreck, as if waiting to be driven somewhere. I waded across the Kain's yard, and with heavy legs, climbed the drowned stairs to the Kain's porch on all fours, like a creature thing; for that porch was above water still. Snake Kain was a little'n them days, 'bout nine. He answered my banging at the porch door, by swiping the steam off the window inside looking out. He shouted of his father.... 'Pappa, Pappa Sir! a n****r just blowed up on to our front porch!.... Pappa, Pappa!' He didn't recognize me I guess, wet overall clinging, caved-over like that, all in a shiver. Old Kain opened the window, enough for his voice to get out, had a voice alright them days.... shouted, 'Git.' I let him know it was Eli.... 'Get your black ass off, over to the parts shed loft boy!' he shouted.... 'Spend the night there.' It was a kind thing Old Kain done me; it saved me from dying of chill or dying of flying metal or dying of plain fright. And there was no getting out that night, and the storm came on fierce; then mighty fierce; and me in that loft there. There were car parts, hub caps, every loose thing pelting that metal shed outside, enough to jump-start a stone-dead man to life; the roof near lifted; I prayed to God.... all that black night long I prayed. As you can see boy, the Lord did answer me....

Quick as it came, water drained from the face of the acres; pools were left between wrecks, pools boiling silver, boiling mad with tiny stranded fish, all in a panic state, all headed to the same fate....a sight Noah must have looked on when that flood fell. I said in my brain, 'Eli, you lucky you didn't get born a fish'; with the mud that settled after, and all the creature life in an upset that-a-way, it was a danger to be about in there amongst the wrecks. The sun soon got to work, digested up every remains of wet, left grey salt mud, cracked and curled and hard like. A stink droned the land.... of all things rotting. In a few months, there was scarce a sign of what past by us, excepting that salt rust began to eat out under each wreck, and show as you see it now boy."

After telling this, Eli walked a slow limp, back along the path he had waded that fierce day, long before ever I was born.

Chapter 13

Eli was now off for a week away, tending his garden of greens and okra, I again was up behind a sorting bin, being grilled and steamed, in massive heat. Luther meantime was out scavenging scrap and automobile parts. "Where's that Luther at?" said Nathan to the air.... "I hate to guess at it," then smiled, as his eyes picked over the land. "We've near about sorted clean out of scrap picking's." It was at this point, all Hell broke free in the place. A voice savaged out from the wrecks.... no mistake.... it was Snake Kain. Nathan listened, head up, his lips half-open like a beaver listens.... the voice of Luther came hard back, there were screams.... again Snake Kain's voice flung out, and Luther's back.... a shot was fired.... Luther, wild-eyed, gripping up his overall straps burst out from the wrecks, blood on neck. Snake, bull-headed, surged after, as Luther took-off at bullet speed, up that soil track. Snake fired twice, but Luther was gone, leaving only raised dust to drift. Seconds later, Young Miss Roxella Kain walked fast in front of our platform with a front-ways stare a queen walk, an up neck, a pout mouth. Snake Kain heaving breaths, bent, yelled after.... "You'll be locked in for keeps now, you daughter-of-a-bitch!" He came close up to the sorting platform, shouted, "One of you bastards must 'a known about this rape.... Caught that son-of-a-bitch pants down black ass in a furious tremble.... about to do its worst, gave that black ass the pistol-thrashing of its life.... if he ever lays foot on this land again, he's a dead n****r." He turned, stormed back to the house, firing two shots into the old Buick as he went.

There was an after-silence, yells from the house, toxic screams, doors thrown shut. Nathan said, "Well boy, if you didn't know it already, you know now, Luther's bin sneakin' off meetin' with Young Miss Roxella Kain, plying her with alcohol, some place out there in the wrecks." For a split moment, I took it for a joke, for Nathan's face was up in a grin; it came serious, my insides fell. "Don't take it hard boy, don't expect he loves her a speck… bet wages on that…. after being thawed out on drink, likely she finds that Luther exitin', him being so buttery with the females, and being as he's the one thing her parents would hate. To Luther, she's just another challenge to his manness and he's had lots of challenges to his manness. She hates his color, and she's attracted more because of it. If it was another man, it might have an ounce of future, but not with Luther. That Luther, I know well, he'll take no heed of threat, or beating or flying lead… he's proud… might be more flying lead over this one before it's done fevered out."

I felt sick, I felt desolate bad, I felt cold under the sun. "Listen boy," said Nathan, "there's a strange thing about hate…. sometimes it breeds the opposite, in spite of itself…. Luther told me yesterday, that Young Miss Roxella got him knees-up sunk in swamp muck after wild iris flowers, shinning up cabbage palms after vine flowers, she shoutin' ' No not that one, THAT ONE!' She's fast getting to own his hide. Kains breed slave bosses in skirt-cloth, well as overalls…. He was loving it that Luther was, she being his biggest challenge, and hoping for a full meltdown…. What that Luther's got, I can only guess at…. in this case…. better not to know it, 'specially if you're heavy tanned."

I sat at the table and stared at the parting on the down-turned head of Young Miss Roxella, trying not to believe. We ate to the sound of forks, till Miss Lorraine skidded back her chair, stood in back of Roxella's, said in a low grave boiling voice, "If you so much as give a sideway look to any of that black scum out there ever again, I'll order up the hiding of your life from Mr Kain, or I'll give it myself…. never mind your age miss. You'll stay indoors permanent now, locked in your room till school."

From now, the only sight I had of Young Miss Roxella was at meals. The white in her eyes chased out by red…. her face a sky about to rain. Beyond this, she was forbidden to leave her room.

"Lafe, Lafe is that you?" the silver voice came through her door. "Lafe," she said, "I must see Luther." I told her he took off sudden, was not expected back ever. "He'll be back, I know it…. Lafe, would you do something for me?" Her voice got golden, "Thieve the ladder from the shed, prop it under my window, the farthest right." "They'll find you out," I whispered. "Don't worry," she said. How could I refuse such a voice? I had snuck out in the early dawn and done it before I had time to think more.

When rain came on, later that day, it came sudden with thunder. The whole afternoon shook, the sorting platform shook. Nathan dropped the scrap he was holding, moved back under the overhang of the iron parts shed. I stood alongside. The electric rain came wicked on, heaviest rain that ever rained…. blue flashes lit the acres of cars in pearly metal light…. steam came up off every dead car roof. We stood, staring out. Hard rain came in ropes down in front of us off the building edge. Out of this blind, Miss Lorraine in apron ran, yelled into the parts shed…… "MR KAIN, MR KAIN!!!!…….. ROXELLA IS BROKEN LOOSE….. IS OUT IN ALL THIS! … FIND THAT GIRL FAST AND NOW!!!!" Snake went careering off through mud and everything, into the wrecks and shouting. Nathan and I ran different directions joining the blinding search. Drenched and bent, I caught glimpses of Snake Kain staggering between rows of wrecks, then out, met me in the yard drawing hard breaths…. "Nothin' boy, nothin'," ….at that we stopped, turned toward a shout. Out of the wrecks a dream shape came, Nathan holding the slack body of Young Miss Roxella Kain. Nathan yelled frantic… "OH LORD IT 'AINT ME DONE IT… SHES'S RATTLESNAKE BIT… SHES BIN BIT BAD!!!!!" Snake Kain ran there, grabbed her out of his arms, as if such black arms had no right touching her. Soon as Snake Kain held the loose shape, Nathan ran, fast as any man could, in splashes away, rain closing behind him.

She lay in a statue way, porcelain, un-moving, beautiful, in the parts shed; clothes clung…. canvas army bed soaking water. Under instruction of Old Mr Kain, Snake had buckled his belt on her leg, few inches up from swollen fang marks. "Not too tight," snapped Old Kain; with her leg drooped down over the cot edge, Snake Kain on all fours, frantic, worked to suck the poison out. In the steam of wet clothes going up, with five Rattlesnake skins nailed to the wall over her, Young Miss Roxella Kain lay, gasping air, in the arms of the death angel.

The lights of the ambulance lit the rain, she was taken. The siren murdered out. I was left standing, heard that siren out, off to the distance, till all was rain noise.

Chapter 14

Next day was grim, not by weather. The sun shone black as Young Miss Roxella Kain lay at the edge of death or life. Snake Kain had questions, first into the face of Nathan. He surged up the sorting platform…. nailed the revolver hard under Nathan's jaw, backed him up, to against the iron building, forcing his head back. "I want words boy…. you two midnights was up to somethin'." Nathan's eyes shot my direction…. "No," said Snake, "it weren't him squealed. Why you run off so hard last afternoon boy? Why you shout out, 'Lord it weren't me done it?'" Nathan forced words, "She be dead now if I hadn't found her sheltered in that Oldsmobile." "That's as maybe, but there's more ain't there boy? …. I seen hate in your eyes for days…. remember boy, I can smell a liar…. You was the arranger of the meet-up between my daughter and Luther weren't you boy, and don't tell me she went out there to pick flowers." Nathan's eyes were wide…. "I never arranged nothing…. she was locked up weren't she? …. how did I know she would break loose…. go in that part?" "What part? …. what d'you mean 'that part?' what part?....spit it out"…. He pressed the gun barrel harder…. "Luther planned it, it weren't nothin' to do with me, all I told him was Young Miss Roxella was locked up for keeps…. I warned him not…. he snuck in, dusk time yesterday, dumped big rattlesnakes, eight or nine, somewhere over that part. Paid a white man plenty for 'em…. laid out two sacks, different places, untied tops and run." "Well why would he do such a thing, right where it's my habit to go shootin' eh boy?.... povidin' me with sport?.... providing me a death bite more like it …. that's it weren't it?.... Miss Roxella took what was meant for me. You two black sons-of-bitches is up for rape and conspiring to murder, and mark me boy,

if my daughter don't pull through, you're a dead n****r. Call
the Sheriff" He shouted at me…. "CALL NOW!" Before I
could get to the parts shed door, two shots exploded out….
Nathan zig zag ran, into the mess of wrecks…. was gone.
That evening I snook in back of the house, saw the ladder
was gone, Miss Roxella must have hidden it back where it
belonged, I heaved a glad breath, crept back to the house.

Two day's on…. Clay smiled…. "She's goin' to pull through
boy." His words were like some bird flew up, dragged the
whole place with it, till he said…. "She might never walk
boy." With this, guilt fell on me…. I was the one after all,
who placed the ladder.

Caloosahatchee Wreckers was as a stopped place in time. No
spares being harvested, no scrap. Snake Kain ordered me to
'Stand ready,' said, "I know which Oldsmobile Miss Roxella
was sheltered at…. there's only one out that part." He wore
mighty thick leather leg protectors, which was not his normal
habit, threw a pair to me. "Wait here boy," he said, as he
waded into weeds between wrecks very wary. After a stretch,
he came out, revolver ready. "Follow me careful." We went
over a car door laid, weeds growing out from the broken
window, over old radiators, past hub-caps stuck in scrub
palmettos, to where a sack lay, open-ended, flat. "There,"
said Snake, "there's the diamondback son-of-a-bitch, in the
back window of that Oldsmobile." It was a window with
no glass. A savage handsome rattlesnake was coiled there.
"Careful boy," he said, "hear that frying bacon sound
boy? That there's the rattle…. got senses sharp as glass….
tongues that taste air…. sure knows we're here…. he's fixin'
to strike." He took slow aim, fired…. its head jolted…. my
ears sang, the job was done. "It'll take a while till its nerves
die-out boy, wouldn't never go pick one up right off, they can
still strike at you out of pure hate." I couldn't help the sad
that came on me as he held it up, "Near six foot," he said
proud. A mighty handsome thing to die, I thought, a mighty
lethal thing to live…. less frightening though than the ugly
man that held it.

He dragged it back to the house, lifted it, dirt covered, said "No skin takin' from this devil boy, couldn't bear to look on it nailed up, remindin' what them black vermin done, if only it was them I got, 'stead of their killing tool…. his coffin boy is the garbage can." He dropped it in.

"This rust farm sure ain't the same place, I left," said Eli when he got back, shock in his eyes. "One week away and all this….if only I'd a 'bin here boy, might have put a manacle on such hot blood….boys get out-o'-line there, this is what happens. When Luther's mamma gets wind of this…. rape, attemptin' murder… going after a white girl…. it'll stab her heart. His mamma's a law and order woman, 'specially in the religious way, but a serious dislike of the white race…. she's proud, proud like her son is….even changed the family name from Oakfield to Ogbomosho, that's some place in Africa….more fittin'…. maybe…. more sayable…. no it 'aint. Better pray this whole thing gets settled peaceful, before there's more flying metal."

"What's your family name?" I said to Eli after a while, as he struggled up parts glued in hard mud, that had been there since that terrible rain day. "Why I'm Pugh, boy, a Pugh, Eli Pugh, and that 'aint no sneeze attack neither! That's my name for lack of any other. Would feel strange to change now anyhow…. For a slave name grows into a family, like a tree grows round an iron nail…. gets to be part of that tree, but it don't never get to be wood."

Snake's orders were on us, to work double hard, double long, 'Till the sun's dead.' Clay was called in, as the getter and bringer of parts and scrap, to keep Eli and me busy, as we sorted in back of the two great wood bins. "Hope this double hard work thing gets double fat pay," said Eli, with a doubting face, as we worked into the long shadows of the day.

I said as we sorted there one day, "How did you get that limpin' leg Eli?" "Well boy, 'bout six year back there, unloading wrecks with Snake; him drivin' that old crane over there, chain slipped, car fell, crushed my leg pretty bad.... fixed me up best they could. Think that Snake had a bit too much of that Blue Ribbon Beer reinforcin' when he fixed that chain on. Still don't blame that boy, sure must be hard to break that drinkin' mould, along with all the other bad moulds he growed into." "I used to think, about that, that blame thing," said Clay, standing smoking nearby. "I was a prison guard a spell over in Broward County there; I used to think, 'if these guys had my Ma and Pa, along with my influences, and me theirs, would they be in my shoes and me theirs'? Are they all victims… some sure must be… are some born plain bad…maybe… can some decide to change…that there must be the hardest of all."

These days were the pattern of our days for many to come, with no sight or sound of Luther or Nathan. "Recon those two took off north to escape the law," said Eli, as we sat one day, staring out, tired to the sinew. Over at the Kain house, a full fuss was on. Miss Lorraine had flower pots out, furniture pieces stood outside; wood floors, wood walls, all scoured germ dead. The smell of disinfectant got hold even to the breakfast grits. A stair-lift was now hurriedly installed, for in two days, Young Miss Roxella would come home.

It was a shake-up for me when I saw her in a wheelchair. I had not expected that the muscle in her leg would be so sunk in, so terrible purple black, the damage so long and deep. As I helped Snake lift her up the porch steps, I could see, some fresh thing had flown out of her. She was changed, and maybe forever, as if she had glimpsed something.

When I came in for dinner late one evening, the meal not yet served; Snake, Young Miss Roxella and Old Kain were already seated at the table. Young Miss Roxella sat, bone-face, bleak in her wheelchair, looked down, stared to the empty plate; her eyes were spoiled by crying. Miss Lorraine sent across anger in a stare toward Roxella. "Happy as usual I see," shouted Miss Lorraine in a rasp voice from the kitchen stove. Snake and Old Kain looked agitated, waiting for food. Roxella yelled back, sudden and furious, "YOU….. YOU DRIED-UP OLD MISERABLE COW, YOU NEVER HAD A HAPPY DAY IN ALL YOUR EXISTIN'" Still with tears, Young Miss Roxella backed-up her wheelchair fast, wheeled herself off. The meal was already done when Roxella came back. She rammed the table leg with her wheelchair, causing a wave of milk to overspill the jug edge. A wisp smile was on her, fixed, her dreamy eyes blinked slow, her eyelashes in clumps from tears. She switched her blunt eyes my direction, warm, as if suddenly she was made of sunshine and sugar. It was as if the roof suddenly lifted off and sun blasted in. "THAT'S HOW IT'S GOIN' TO BE NOW IS IT?" fired Miss Lorraine, eyes narrowed, staring furious. With rough hands, Miss Lorraine backed the wheelchair, pushed Roxella fast to the stair-lift, hitting the door-frame on the way. Snake and Old Kain had already left. I sat a moment in some warm afterglow, but with a faint after-smell of gin. How could something so unsweet have sweetened her so? Was this sweet Roxella the true Roxella?

As weeks passed, except for Sunday church, Young Miss Roxella never would leave the house; would speak but few words only at meals, and those words had an angry spiteful tinge. Most times she sat in her wheelchair on the porch, staring endlessly out; as if watching for somebody, as the metal rusted before her endless eyes.

Chapter 15

The summer heat droned on. August came fierce and sticky, air like syrup. Every afternoon after three, gray clouds would sulk the sky over, make what Miss Lorraine called, 'A Confederate Sky': Confederate guns, Confederate drum rolls sounded off at a distance from fat clouds. Miss Lorraine would lift her face before it, drink the wind. To my ear and eye, it was something threatening always, though oftentimes there was no rain to back the threat. Some evenings, the beams and slats of that old wood house would shake from thunder, as surely as any line of cannon could have made it. Young Miss Roxella stayed melancholy through storms and summer days. Her eyes stared always. When I did manage to say off a handful of words to her at breakfast or dinner, no change came to her stare.

It was on one of these hot pressing Confederate afternoons, that from the yard we workers saw a commotion at the Kain house. Old Kain could not swallow food or get breath. The ambulance came. He was already done for, there was no reviving that tough old man. A Sunday gloom came over the place, a gloom that outdid any clouds or rain. For good or bad, an era was fading. What might happen from here was frightening even to me.

The funeral was seen-to and done without us workers. As time passed we got word whispered through Clay that Old Kain had stored up a little fortune, and it fell on the pockets of Snake and Miss Lorraine Kain. Aside from money, they were left the Southern Kain's half of the scrap business and land.

At night there was bitter shouting, Snake getting drunk, Miss Lorraine saying…. "I'm not about to see you liquidate the inheritance down the toilet."…. Him yelling, "Might as well, you old battle bag, before you bet it all away on the dogs!" This was the first time I ever heard Snake Kain stand up against Miss Lorraine to her face.

Further word came that Miss Lorraine and Young Miss Roxella were leaving 'right soon' for Tupelo Mississippi and would not be back. Divorce papers would be filed, fast as lawyer, ink and paper could be forced together.

Breakfast the next day was a rushed thing, Miss Lorraine banging a plate hard on the table in front of Snake. "It's the last breakfast you'll get from these hands," was all she said. I ate my grits wordless, opposite Young Miss Roxella.

A moving van arrived. Most of the furniture and the best set of dishes went, Young Miss Roxella's piano, that I never saw her sit at went. There was no Snake to watch them away. He lay in a drunk state on the army cot in the parts shed. Young Miss Roxella was dressed white, beautiful, as when I first saw her. As they started away, Miss Loraine did not look at me, or look to the house she had known for those many years, the years and me were already behind her. Young Miss Roxella managed a weak hand moving… they were gone!

I saw no sign of Snake Kain all morning, and for need of some better thing, I did work. Snake did not show up all afternoon or evening either. The next morning I saw the pickup truck was gone. 'He's gone after Miss Lorraine' was my first thought.

Chapter 16

A few hours beyond morning, a run of explosions corrugated the sticky air. A motorcycle exploded into the yard. Snake Kain was a matched twin to his new bought Harley Davidson motorcycle, black it was. He revved it, he grinned evil, he revved again, reared it up. Eli, Clay and myself stood amazed. "I'm surprised he chose black," said Eli with half a laugh. He skidded about the dirt like a child pretending. He was fitted up in black leather and sweating in it; had black gloves with no finger ends, had a red bandana tied on his greasy head, had the look of the vermin of the land there, as he revved, exploded off to the house.

It was a few days after that I stumbled across Snake Kain, up early, downing, un-heated, the last can of beans and bacon, left in the wake of Miss Lorraine's leaving. He had pain in his forehead from his night before thing, but got out a few words, head down, hair down over the open can. "You ain't never seen the outside of this place have you boy, excepting for church going? We're meetin' up with Clay, pick you up round four." Before I knew what, I was gripping the back of his leather jacket…. we flew out from there….Confederate cannon booming far off. Into known territory we roared, then out, followed some railroad tracks, past an army navy store, past a farm feed store, past broken windows and boarded shops, to a place called, 'The North Side Drive-In.' A girl, a scraggy girl with glasses, took three dollars from Snake, told him what station to tune his radio to. We drove to a field in front of a giant curved screen. Cicada noise from a nearby tree surged, then whispered down to an idle drone, as people sprawled on grass in back of their pickup trucks.

There were people in sleeping bags in spite of the heat, dogs lying disinterested, and every kind of picnic eating going on.

We met Clay, sitting, his back to the fender of his pickup truck. "Hope you've got a radio Snake, or this here'll be a silent picture show," said Clay. Snake hauled up a radio from one saddle-bag, a twelve-pack of beer from the other. In little time they had finished off three cans each, were on the next. A black family pulled alongside, set themselves out on a blanket. "Let's move," Snake said…. "bad enough having to work with 'em, but I won't sit alongside of no monkeys." Two little girls their hair divided out in many braided partings, wearing white cotton dresses, rolled on the grass, rolled dangerously close to Snake, their voices like silver bells, as their parents sat laying out a small white table-cloth, setting out food from a basket. "Come on boys, let's move, I can't stand the sight of it," said Snake. "You can move if you want to Snake, they don't bother me any; anyhow you won't notice 'em soon as the movie starts up," said Clay.

Snake kept jabbing his sight across at them, as he tipped his head back to finish the bottom of the can. After another empty hit the grass, Snake said to Clay, "If my Great, Great Grandfather Wade Kain could see this here, he'd raise-up in his gray uniform, out from the dirt, holler, and rail and smite all you n****r nanny liberals, that what he fought against come to this. Call yourself a Southerner do you?" "Look Snake," said Clay, "I was grown here just like you was, my Great, Great Grandfather fought for the Confederacy, same as yours…..only mine died for it. I have his handed-down diary…. it ends sudden one day. There's not a word about fighting to keep fat gutted plantation owners in slaves. He fought and died because we was invaded by bluebelly scum…. violatin' our women, firing our homes, spilling our blood, and carrying-off every animal and crumb. You never knowed any blacks personal, except to work under you as semi-slaves did you Snake?" Snake roared, getting to shaky legs…. yelled, "You're the type of Southerner who's let the

South get to a second class place and stay there…. you love n****rs don't you?…. I've seen you out in the yard." As this boiled, the black family fired disturbed looks our way.

From alcohol oiled tongues, their anger grew…. exploded, they came surging, fists raised I stood between, felt strange to be there. I was rescued, when the black family moved quickly. Snake and Clay slacked off their anger, lay silent. As country songs went over us, more beer went into us, the screen lit alive with advertisements in front of us. The film was 'The Last Picture Show,' but what it was about, I lost mostly. It was a Southern town in the 1950's, that's all I could say as solid fact; except for the huge sight, when the girl on the screen took off her top in the pickup truck. This did a good job taking their anger off, uniting them, saying, 'Corrrr….look at them rocks!' In the dusk light, Snake stood in the shadow against the truck, emptied himself of used beer, made a lot of noise doing it. To the giant country sound of Loretta Lynne, and giant people eating popcorn on the screen, the show ended. Snake said goodbye to Clay with a violent back slap. We roared on out from there.

Chapter 17

Through weeks of nightmare nights, I kept hope for better nights. Snake would arrive to the Kain house late, with every kind of thing that would plug in and make wild noise: radios, record-players, electric guitars, electric drums, never food. He did not lack for drink. An entire juke-box arrived by truck one afternoon…. that house shook to the earth under it. Nights were Hell nights, drunken party nights till day. At first I tried to join-in, but after being punched by a leather-wearing woman, and coming across more brawling women, that pawed me…. witches with axel grease on their eyes, I stuck to my room; got sleep in bits, between roars, between yells, sometimes gun shots, and sometimes thumps against my door. In the morning I would pick my way out, past and over sleeping people. There some mornings would be Snake Kain, flat lying, in the middle of his new friends, gut rising. Often times new-bought radios or televisions were left …. insides kicked out. I was kept sane by Eli and Clay, who joked, "Guess Snake didn't care for the program on T.V…. Snake'll flame hi'self out pretty soon now boy," said Eli, "all you have to do is survive it"

Eli and Clay both gave a firm black oil handshake and a good slap on the shoulder, when my sixteenth birthday arrived. I had begun to notice a change in them. Clay would ask…. "How about if I work over that area today?" and Eli, "When should we have Clay haul the bin of cast aluminum, it's getting mighty heaped?" Before I knew, they had me trained-up running the place. Orders for parts coming in, better wages paid out.

Snake Kain had started his new money life from a low rung on the health ladder, he stared in a dead-man stare; he was all but used-up, his inheritance spent-up. On a quiet September morning, a Saturday, I found Snake Kain outside the parts shed door in the dirt, shaking, lying, a beer can still in his big grip hand. He heard me, half got up, staggered, shook with waves of shaking, fell back. I got him to his army cot in the parts shed. He stank of rot more than ever he had. I started to panic, showed it. He grabbed my overall front as I laid him down, whispered, "I forbid such things as doctors.... Now swear to me boy on your mother's grave, (which upset me more) not to get no doctor nor nothin'." At the house, I searched the knife drawer, found the address Miss Lorraine had stuffed there on her leaving day. "Butcher Residence," the maid said. I left word that Mr Kain was on the edge of death... Miss Lorraine should come at once.

In bursts of staggers and stumbles I got Snake across the dirt yard to his room and bed. Snake was far from being an easy patient, often times he would throw the soup at me that Eli had brought.... shouting, 'Horse piss.' I felt like leaving him to die, the miserable animal. On Tuesday, out from a taxi got Miss Lorraine, wearing a fine travelling dress.... a straw hat.... hat pins through it. She stood, we looked at each other a long moment. She said, "Well mercy boy, stop starin', you've certainly grown some." Her eyes swerved past me to the house, to the litter of beer cans all about on the earth.... Miss Lorraine had somehow got a slight waist to her body, on account of a belt she had squeezed herself with. She had an accent stretched like chewing gum, with soot on her eyelashes, flour on her cheeks, she looked like an antique rescued. "Where's Mr Kain at boy?" "Still laid-up in the bedroom .... still no better," I said. One of her high heeled shoes jabbed through the rotted deck boards just then, on her way in. I had to yank her shoe out, handed it to her. She said "On my foot boy," as she wobbled, gripped the doorway edge. I struggled that shoe back on her fat foot. This was a re-treaded and re-conditioned Miss Lorraine for sure.

Inside she undid her hat, handed it to me, along with gloves. Lacking a hook, I dropped them on the greasy table. "Send that man Eli in," she said, looking at the wreck of her kitchen that now was. Eli was amazed at seeing the inside of a house he had never set foot in all the many years. He had a puzzled look, an uncomfortable look, as he glanced at the ceiling boards, at the state of mess before him. He did a slight bow, and as she spoke, he made small bows, as if they were commas in her commands…. followed up with, "Yes Ma…am, Miss Lorraine." He looked delighted with the way she was turned-out, he grinned. "Eli, I want all the outside cleared of debris… do you have any women at home who are industrious about a house?" "I'm a man living alone Miss Lorraine, but I'll find help…. it sure looks like that's what you'll be needin'." "Enough of that…. see to it Eli and bring in my trunk. You boy fill in for Mr Kain, temporary, while he is indisposed, now boy inform Mr Kain of my arrivin'." She stood in the doorway of the bedroom, after being announced, Snake with wide eyes stared. "Mr Kain, it was only by considerable urging on the part of Roxella alone that I am here, soon as you are in a mended state, I expect to depart to civilization…. you understand?" Snake just nodded from the bed. With him still in a state of big eyes, I closed the door as we left.

"The spare room is to be my room for this brief visit boy, instruct Eli to telephone the help, they are needed sooner than at once. I must have that room decent before tonight." What she ordered was done.

Chapter 18

Over the next few days, Miss Lorraine strutted about the place; soon the house was bullied into germ-free order. The old stove rubbed to a state of black it had never seen, the table scoured raw, waxed and brought new, lamp shades new, stair carpets new; the outside, painted to white, almost as pure as the old wood church.

None of this was by the muscle-work of Miss Lorraine. Often times, she sat on the front porch, cooling her face with a piece of ice in a cloth, issuing commands, or chasing the help. I went back to working. The two new black boys we hired, learned to sort scrap well from Eli, everyone knew his job and did it. I began to feel like one of the spare parts laying about in the parts shed. Is this how Snake Kain must have felt?

It was getting to be fall, Snake Kain was slow to recover, he seemed happy under the steel hand of his former wife. One evening Miss Lorraine and myself sat down to dinner, served by the black maid. Miss Loraine dismissed her early saying "Selma, we are over-full and not in a state for dessert." Snake was as usual sleeping. "Boy," said she, "I never told you, that your Pappa owned half this establishment, and it's fallen to you." I managed a look of surprise. "Wouldn't you like to go back to Ohia with $5000 in your pocket? Think what you could do with that money? It's for your half of this business and land. That's an offer on the generous side boy," she said, eyebrows up. $5000, it was a fortune, she could see it by my face…. "Go think on it boy, it's a wonderful offer."

I was distracted by money thoughts, thoughts that I might never see Young Miss Roxella again if I accepted it. All the night through and into the next day it orbited my brain. Eli cut his finger deep on a generator housing that I was supposed to be holding down for him. "What's the matter boy, you're half off someplace," said Eli. "I'm real sorry Eli," I said, "You'd better go wash that cut at the drinkin' fountain in back of the parts shed." Eli sucked his finger, said, "I ain't never been allowed to that drinkin' water here, guess the Kains was worried the black might rub off, or some such thing idea." "I'm in temporary charge now Eli, official from Miss Lorraine, so go do it." But he wouldn't, he wouldn't break a rule put there by Old Mr Kain so long ago.

I told Eli of Miss Lorraine's offer of $5000. Eli settled the palm of his hand round his chin. "Well boy, that is a puzzlement ain't it. Clay told me that Miss Lorraine just two days ago, bought Snake's QUARTER part off of him for $5000." I looked disbelieving. "No wonder she came here so fast." "So," said Eli, "I would say you owning HALF, she's either over generous to her one-time husband, or under generous to you boy. Look I know a man at my church who could put a real value on this land, just leave it in my hands." When the answer came back from Eli that the total land was worth $30,000 and my half $15,000, I almost fainted right then in the yard. Two days after I was coming in from work, saw Miss Lorraine sitting on the new front porch swing. She said, with a point face, head tilting.... "Thought about my offer boy?" I had serious nerves right then, blurting the real value of the land and how I knew it. She stood, came angry, lost her culture. "Rubbish, it ain't worth nowhere near about that, you've been led wrong boy. Why did you go jabberin' your mouth off? Ooooh that n****r Eli, I'll have hard words with that Eli over this." I watched her stride across to where Eli was getting set to leave for the day. She stood, feet wide like a chair. Though I couldn't get the words, it was plain she was mighty angry. She trod back to the house in her old-style Miss Lorraine bossy walk, told me Eli was given his walking papers. I felt terrible sick over it.

Chapter 19

The place felt emptied without Eli, even though Clay did his best to cheer me, the guilt I felt over Eli weighed on my mood every waking second. It was in the two weeks following, that Snake Kain started to pick-up old habits. He went rattlesnake killing one time, jump-started his drinking by getting seriously drunk, yelled at the two new metal sorters we had trained up. One day one was gone…. soon both. More were hired…. these were bad learners, cast aluminum, brass, copper wire, sorted wrong. At day's end, I had to re-sort the days sorting. Eli sent word through Clay he was happy doing gardening work, had grown the best collard greens, on God's land… 'Good enough to make a man HOLLA!' he hoped to see me soon.

Cooler weather made an end to Confederate skies and mosquitoes. My mood lifted when Clay said, "Boy, that Young Miss Roxella is expected any day now." That magical girl still haunted my brain, haunted the whole Kain place, especially whenever I looked off from the metal sorting platform to where she once stood… electric blue sash, white cotton dress, as alive in my head as if she was standing right there. She now took up my thoughts…. even blocked away some of the guilt I felt over Eli, the fresh beautiful winter days made her image strong.

But daydreams and hard daylight are often times much different. I watched the taxi to a standstill over at the Kain house, checked my face in a car wing mirror, rubbed the grease off my hands, mostly, arrived at the taxi on weak legs. "Hello Lafe," she said in a paper-thin voice. Her looks had faded, but there were flashes of magic…. her lilt of voice, the edge of her mouth as she made a faint smile, or the sudden shift of her eyes. But she was quite snappy with the taxi driver, as he and I struggled her up the porch steps. The breath of her hair on my neck as we put her into her wheelchair, shivered a spirit through me, though her true breath was of a different spirit. She hardly gave a second look my direction after that, preferring to fuss over the stair-lift, the lack of drawer space in her room. As time slid, there were days at the table, in her wheelchair, that Young Miss Roxella took on a soft contented warm state of mood. At these times, I wanted just to hold her, hug her, if only for the tick of a clock. But other times when a full sulk was on her, her eyes took a turn of look so cold she could frost-up a room; right after, she could fire up with fury at the smallest thing. It was hard to know which Roxella would show; hard to know which Roxella was the true Roxella.

One afternoon I noticed the black maid Selma, returning from a grocery trip, she put one brown grocery bag separate. The chinking as she carried it to Young Miss Roxella's room was enough said. The discovery of empty gin bottles at the back of the house confirmed the sad truth.

On an evening, the last light falling, Young Miss Roxella guided her wheelchair to where I sat on the porch. She smiled softly, beautifully, said, "To sit here, have no mosquitoes, why it's luxury Lafe." I saw she had pointy looks pressing through her soft face. She was now less distant, as if her terrible leg, had, by making her less perfect, made her more human. She stared to the last of the light, said, "I never thanked you for placing the ladder Lafe." "Why would you thank me for that? …. look what happened to you." She quick pulled the blanket to hide her poor damaged leg. "I know you hated to know I was seeing Luther, and, if I'm not mistaken, I know how you felt toward me. You placed that ladder in spite and because of that." I came over red-faced, switched my look to away. "I have something I must discuss Lafe." My heart took off…. crashed as she said, "It's about the land…. Our family has lived on this land three generations. My Grandpa and a bunch of n****rs cleared this land, cut the slash pines off it, pulled the stumps, worked this business thirty years. I would say that makes the land and business ours, wouldn't you? Your father put money in at the beginning to help buy the land, never worked the land, never sweat its sun, never knew it's animals, it's flowers, yet your family maintained it was theirs equally. Your father even told us we paid too little to the black workers; we were near to slave holders, while at the same time sharing in the profits of that so called slavery. When you think of my mother's offer, weigh it, weigh it Lafe. Her offer is generous, and more than that." That tune of voice she had came as if out from the throat of a white oleander flower, so fresh so pure, so beautiful it's tune; it seemed to put back all the beauty that injury and time had taken; yet I knew she was sent by Miss Lorraine. I loved being with her, but I had to get away, for, as the angel-like oleander flower, there was something poisonous in her right then.

I dithered about, one day I wouldn't sell, next day I would. I'd decide the southern Kains HAD rights to my half through hard labor, though I had seen little of that from Snake, then worried on that I was being robbed. I saw in some thinking, my mother, father, grandfather.... what would they do?

Without Eli here, I was lost. It was good to have my thinking broken by Clay, who turned up driving the old truck. He said, "Well boy, this 'eres a tricky one.... I see both sides. Maybe there ARE rights of owning by sweat, but if I was put where you're standin' I don't recon I could take being forced out of it 'specially by a force in the shape of Miss Lorraine. Maybe she'll up her offer to a more good-looking one."

Monday morning, Miss Lorraine was in the pickup truck, being driven by the black maid Selma, as I understood intending going hat shopping. I sat on the bottom rung of the sorting platform steps. She yelled the maid to a stop by me, got out, stood, trussed up, high rigged, looked down at me, "Well?" she said, "Well?" I looked to the dirt, shook my head. "That's it is it?" her voice final. "Let's get it clear then shall we boy…. your half lies to that side…. your half runs from that gate-post left, along the far side of the driveway, clear over to that dead tree distant. Take my offer as it stands, or you'll take your land as it lies, and carry the burden of the $250 taxes yearly with it. If you don't like how it's divided up…. sue me boy !…. I'll see you gone from the house by tomorrow, less'n you want to pay rent on your room…. Do a boy a good turn…. he turns this-a-way, and bites at you!" She climbed back into the pick-up truck, slammed the door, made motion to Selma to drive on out.

I stood on the Kains dirt drive, looked at my inheritance. It was a sad sight, rust and twisted dead to far off, all well scavenged. Above the rest, a lone yellow school bus lay, its hood lifted. I trod to it slow, carful. I was careful too, to check out the insides with a piece of long pipe, for it looked like snake territory. This, I was made to decide, was my new home. I carried my few things across from the Kain house, hid my Ohio box under the driver's seat. There I spent the night, to the sound of cotton rat's feet across the bus roof. The lights of the Kain house shone lonely out, I slept little that long night.

Chapter 20

When word got out of my isolation, Eli was soon sitting alongside of me, in front of that old yellow school bus, that itself sat wheel-high in weeds and palmettos. "Brought you a bus warmin' gift," said Eli with that big smile. He jabbed open a can with a knife, cooked bacon and beans in a hubcap on an open fire. As Eli laid down two battered tin plates and spoons, said, "We can make it work boy, if you want it to, you might get enough even to pay the taxes, at least for this year." At that moment, as we lay there on weeds, anything seemed possible. "We'll harvest the parts there is, I can haul them along with any scrap in my pickup…. I've got good contacts out there boy." I lay comfortable that night on my bed of moldy bus seats, thinking on Eli and me.

I woke sudden, to the sound of a truck, men shouting, metal poles being slid. Miss Lorraine had hardened her heart more. Inside a day, a six-foot-high chain-link fence was taking shape; inside a week, I was cut off from the Southern Kains. The ugly fence that Miss Lorraine caused to grow, staggered the land in zigzag shape, far to the distance, to the end of five acres. The thought that I was now cut off from ever seeing Young Miss Roxella, hurt more than any other thing.

Eli and I worked with nothing but a wrench, our hands, a rusted chain and Eli's old pick-up truck. We dragged cars to one side, cleared a driveway in, dragged clear a yard in front of the school bus, built a sorting platform and bins out of old pallets. Clay was our only link now with the Southern Kains.

Eli came every day except Sundays. The business was planted by hard work, though the harvest was pitiful small. Still it started to feel like the best days, Eli was my friend and family mixed into one. The money we made we shared. We were drinking coffee one day, staring out through the ugly fence to the now weed-grown sorting platform over at the Southern Kain's place, I said to Eli, "Let's have it written up on paper Eli, you and me business partners."

 Eli looked taken by surprise, looked embarrassed, wiped the sweat off his forehead, "No boy, I's just helpin' you out till you gets firm on your feet... I got too many miles on this old milometer.... Anyway, there's okra, beans and corn to plant." "Look Eli, we share work, we share money already, why not?" "I'd feel like a man in a wool suit on a hot day, no.... no boy, you be the boss of your own world." I knew from some tone, a tone I had heard whenever he had spoken to Old Mr Kain, that this was 'talking to the white'. We found a lawyer, papers were drawn up, Eli wearing a suit and looking prickly hot, signed 'Eli Whitney Pugh' along side of me. We shook a firm handshake.

Next day, I said, "Eli Whitney... wasn't that the cotton gin inventor?" "Yeh boy, when I was first hatched there, in 1929, my mamma and poppa was hoping I'd be nudged towards a mechanical sort of bent.... famous inventor side they was hopin' I guess. They never knew that there cotton gin was so good at separatin' seed from cotton balls, it called for thousands more pickin' slaves to feed it. Only thing I've invented boy, is a way of survivin' under them Southern Kains." Eli took a handful of that dry, sandy soil, let it spill from his old fist. "They tell me this land used to be cattle country, boy, 'stead of wreck country. Cattle from here was shipped north, kept the Confederate Army in meat and drippin'....way long before it kept Southern Kains in scrap and grease! There's a lot of people history here, right under our feet."

As the year worked forward, Eli looked happier than I had ever seen him, even amongst clouds of summer mosquitoes. "Man them people biters sure getting' fierce again boy," he said, rubbing off each arm, that left streaks of bright red on dark skin. Some days we heard shots from Snake Kain's Civil War revolver, at the far other side of the fence. Some days we heard helicopter noise come thumping in low and terrible loud, like the passing of the shadow of an angel over us, dropping mosquito larvicide. Eli and I took fast shelter in the bodies of cars, poison rain fell past window holes, dead cars were caused to shudder from the massive noise, as if started up a moment; as if all was as it once was, the father the mother in front, kids in the back. "That poison sure packs a powerful bad smell," yelled Eli one day, "It's a close weigh-up between being poisoned dead or being blood-drained dead by mosquitas'." But when the sleeping sickness was about, the Encephalitis disease, and fear of being given it from mosquitoes, the scales tipped in favor of being poisoned.

At full summer, I could see through the fence, the small outline of Young Miss Roxella, as she sat staring from her high-up dormer window, staring past each day…. day on day the same till full summer turned to late summer. It was then that dragonflies came in millions across the acres, they made sudden turns, weaving over the wrecks. "Now there's a sight I'd pay to see," said Eli.

All through the days the mosquitoes were eaten by dragonflies, and the face of the land was dark with eaters. When clouds got lumpy, when blue was forced out from the sky by a gray Confederate sky, those eaters came on mighty thick, till hardly a mosquito was left to know the world.

It was one of those dragonfly days that Eli shouted "Mosquito killer, malathion," two pure white DC-3 planes came thundering mighty low, like the coming of the world's ending, they gassed our air with clouds of rolling poison. Fast, we shut ourselves in the school bus, Eli said, "Snake always loved it when they did this fogging, as a little'n he'd even run out in it, dance around in it, maybe that's why he took to pestering us, and balling us out so…. pesticide on the brain!" All that sad afternoon, our million dragonflies, skidded upside-down across car roofs, flew at us in insane flight, they dropped poisoned-mad and dead all at one go. "The fools have killed the eaters," shouted Eli, "We'll have a mosquito plague on us after this,"…. and we did.

I was unable to contact Young Miss Roxella through all that sticky summer. The sight of her at her high up window, kept her always in front of my thoughts. I gave Clay a note to deliver to her, telling her of my feelings, asking hers, but there was never a reply. In these late September days, Eli would often times arrive with muscadine grapes, watermelon, or boiled green peanuts, all planted and raised by his old fingers. "Never tasted anything so good!" I said as we finished up the last of the peanuts. "You gets out of soil what you puts in boy, people, peanuts, it's all the same!"

The money we made, we split in wages Eli and I…. most of Eli's, alongside of mine, I hid away in my Ohio box, which itself I hid under the bus driver's seat. Hard times were in the air for the whole country…. people losing jobs. By the strange nature of the trade, we prospered. People turned to using used parts to save money; it got to where we couldn't keep up. We felt rich beyond imagining, had already saved over $9,800, my Ohio box was bursting, tied closed. Sudden, as if the whole country closed their wallets, it all ended, need for parts withered, scrap prices fell…. Eli and I fell back on eating collard greens and ham-hocks. "Cheapest thing since Manna fell on them Israelites," said Eli, wiping off his mouth with the back of his hand.

The dreadful news that Clay was deadly sick, we got late. Eli heard word from Clay's sister, telling of the encephalitis. He had been in Lee Memorial Hospital two weeks. Soon we were standing next to Clay's bed. "He will pull through it" said the nurse, "but if he'd been your age or yours," pointing to Eli and I "He'd have most likely been gone, for it's usually the old and young that gets a ticket to God from that brain inflaming disease." Eli and I gulped. "Boys," Clay managed to say, "lately Miss Lorraine's business is hurting bad. Before I got mosquito bit, two weeks back, I heard Miss Lorraine talk of selling up…. no money around these days. But before you get glad over it, on top she said, 'I won't sell to that Northern boy person and his n****r no matter what!" As Eli and I gave a forced cheerful goodbye to Clay, he said, "By the way boy, I tried to deliver your letter to Young Miss Roxella, Miss Lorraine intercepted me, ripped it out of my hand, ripped it up."

"It's up for sale! Eli shouted in the bus door…. "The Kains' is up for sale for sure boy." I ran to the gateway, Eli limping after, there we both stared amazed. A real-estate sign…. 'Five Acres: Multiple Use: $15,000.'

"Why, don't that beat the pants off a pig," was all Eli managed to say right then.

Chapter 21

On an afternoon, that same late summer, the lid of heaven took on a doleful mood…. a blue-black stain spread the sky over…. wind got-up wild. What came on, out-did all I have ever seen. From that sky dropped a black line, a snake that twisted, danced before the scenery of cars; that came murdering forward out of the north; scattering, ripping, exploding at the back of our five acres. Both Eli and I ran for his truck. "THE KAINS!" shouted Eli, as we did a sharp hook turn at the driveway end, into the Southern Kains.

We burst into the Kain's house, found Miss Lorraine in the kitchen, high-necked, shocked, mending her face by make-up. I ran double steps up the staircase, Eli followed, found Young Miss Roxella at her window, staring fixed out at what was coming. We seized her up, between us we brought her out. With Miss Lorraine still protesting, we managed to get her and Roxella into the truck fast, the last desperate thing Eli did, was to drag Snake Kain off his cot, in the parts shed, struggled him across the dirt, threw him onto the bed of Eli's truck. With Miss Lorraine, Roxella and Eli in the cab, me on the back with Snake flat on his back, gut juddering, we sped out from there down the dirt track and away. Last thing I saw at a distance…. that fence, being ripped out by its roots, spun up high, like a ladder to Hell.

We went but one mile, pulled in at the white painted church: It shone out hard white, a pure thing, against that blue-black sky. From there we watched the tornado take a path, slow and slantwise across toward the south, slaughtering the land. As it headed off, two fire trucks hurtled down past the church, in the direction of the Kain's place. Their sirens sounded forever out, as they were slowed by debris. There was smoke that swirled up, far off, being chopped flat by wind. "Oh Lord not the house!" Miss Lorraine cried. She dropped to her knees before the white church spire, rose prayers before it; but those prayers too seemed cut to bits, strung off away by the gale.

Half an hour later, at the badgering of Miss Lorraine, we started on back, slow toward the Kains. The way was scattered mad with every kind of thing. Telephone poles leaned, car fenders, mudguards trapped up in wires. A snake hung slack dead on a power line. The air was loaded with smell, black smoke fogged the path we steered. As we pulled into the Kain's long driveway, the sight before us, none was prepared for. The fence was all but gone, cars were drifted in piles and lay in every angle, as if raked by a hand. The Kain's parts shed roof ripped open like a knifed can…. and the saddest of all sights…. the Kain house, burning still, with only the naked brick chimney thrusting like an arm and fist, up out of gray ash and flame.

We looked upon the sight without words. It was as if a hard fight had gone on, sky had fought the land, and all the human world between, in harm's way. I saw through smoke, the old school bus, stuck upwards, where it had landed nose down, as if dropped that way by a hand out from clouds. Firemen fought fires that ran out fierce, storms of sparks went up, as automobile radiators boiled and blew up. In the midst of all, the live oak, ripped, broken, with a tire hung on one good limb, defiant standing. It wasn't long before smoke switched to our way, so as to make breathing and seeing a trouble. Young Miss Roxella's eyes teared, from smoke or upset, it could not be told. Tires burned, the sun went black. We left from there, still silent…. each of us now with an altered future to look to.

Miss Lorraine and Young Miss Roxella went by taxi to 'civilization' to a hotel in town. Snake set off on foot to a bar, saying, 'No' to offers of sleep under Eli's roof. Eli took me to his small wood house, where I slept on the floor. All that night, blown smoke dreams passed through me. I saw the school bus, high up floating slow down, out of a blue-black sky. My mother's picture along with $10,000 scattered to the wind in the tempest.

I woke tired, to the Sunday smell of breakfast biscuits being baked by Eli, and the black radio station.... "Sisters and brothers gather round your radio cabinets.... for 'The Hour of Miracles' is upon us." Then the song I had heard Eli so often hum.... "For I'll r-i-s-e again....I'll r-i-s-e again.... death won't keep me in the ground." Eli sat in front of the kitchen stove, Bible rested on the flat of one hand. He made a shape there, of Sunday calm. "This Bible book boy.... it's the best chapter book a man can read-on." He closed it slow, said.... "Here take it.... it's yours boy. Through level and steep, it'll keep your tread true." Looking at it, I was humbled, for this was his own family Bible. "I never had a son," said Eli... "Not another word," was all else said.

Chapter 22

Everywhere smelled burned, everything soot, as we stood, Eli and I in the Sunday light. The Kain's side had places not touched, others mangled to mad. In the parts shed, covered in damp, Snake Kain lay, his revolver trapped in the bend of his arm, as if his only last friend. "Must have found his way back in the night," Eli whispered, "Gone sleepin' starin' to the stars out of that ripped open roof." He seemed in his usual drunk coma, snorting noise. It was something near to comforting, to see him unchanged, in a changed world. We turned our eyes to our destroyed acres.

"Money ain't nothing boy, compared to havin' two arms, two legs and a breathing head," Eli said, for he could read my face, I had turned it with dread the direction of the yellow school bus, stuck end-up at an angle. "We'll dig her out boy, don't worry a snap, we'll dig her out along with that cash money…. we will boy." The settled feeling I got from Eli's words soon fell off as I saw nearer to the bus. The door was gone, the engine crushed back into the drivers part; the seat, the driver's seat, under which my Ohio box was always hidden, ripped from its bolts, stuck against the roof. My secret hiding place lay told…. empty!

I scrambled to the door. Eli shouted, "No boy!" as he tried to grab me back by my overall straps. I searched about a good long while, till creaking noises scared me out. My box, my mother's picture, the only physical picture I had of her, all my Ohio treasures, all our $10,000 all my so hard earned five cents gone!

The next day through, and the next, we labored, Eli and I.

We righted the school bus, using Eli's pickup truck, ropes, chains and sweat. We had no word or knowledge of Miss Lorraine or Young Miss Roxella. Snake Kain had deserted his army cot in the parts shed. The remains of hope I had of finding my Ohio box in that bus was lost. As I searched I found only my old cardboard suitcase, my Ohio outfit in it mildewed, but nowhere the box!

In the days that followed, Eli and I searched. Under every wreck we moved, was disappointment....yet we looked, still we hoped. On an afternoon late, Eli limped up to me all in a shake, "Boy," he said, catching air.... "I was searching over that side, near a tire pile there.... One of them gray critter cotton rats, 'bout that size, spranged out at me.... ran up my overall leg to about half way.... took a leap off into nothin'....then hobbled off.... fat it were....slow for a rat." He rested his hand on my shoulder, caught more air. "There be no creature walking God's good land that gives me a panic sweat quicker than one of them gray rats do." Eli spent what was left of the day getting back calm.

All the remains of the week, we looked, Eli and I, disturbing worms, bull ants out of their new homes. "We be destroyers of their rightful living places now boy.... they sure adapt to change, not like us humans," said Eli.... "But they're mighty roaring mad about being disturbed," and they were mighty mad, 'specially much those bull ants; the soldiers of their race were big, were fighting men, ready for a brawl anytime, many a chopping bite Eli and I got at the jaws of them.

Like bull ants ourselves, we gave all fight and muscle to our task, till the walking-dead stage, only then to slide our backs down against the door of some old wreck, crumpled like that. "Two facts laid side by side," said Eli.... "Your box gone.... Snake Kain gone. Suppose Snake Kain picked over the bus wreck, first light that Sunday, before we got there?" I had a picture straight then.... Snake Kain greasing off, my Ohio box under his evil arm. At this actual moment, he could be standing, filtering our Ohio box money through his nasty intestines.

Chapter 23

As the work went, as days brightened and dimmed, Eli tried to settle my upset, to say there was the hand of God in it; but I had a thorn in my forehead about it…. Hope rusted to no hope, the cash money and my Ohio things lost for keeps. As the late sun slanted on one of these despairing days, I stood messed in soot, wipes of it, smears of it. I got sight of a person at Kains side, wheeling a bicycle, I yelled; he picked his way holding a telegram. It read, 'WILL SELL MY HALF TO YOU stop FIFTEEN THOUSAND DOLLARS NO LESS stop' and an address in Tupelo Mississippi, signed Miss Lorraine Butcher Kain. How on God's land can I buy it off her, my first thought; did I want it? …. my second.

Next day I cleaned myself up at Eli's; brushed down my Ohio outfit as best could be. When Eli and I arrived at the bank, Eli was careful to hide himself and his pickup truck at the far part of the bank parking lot. The man eyed me head to boots, he had pencil point eyes …. his office smelled of money and soap. "Take a seat," he said, meanwhile hinging back on his chair, balanced like a scale, he looked above my head, twiddled his pen, while hearing my request for a loan, all the while weighing. "This is not usual boy, for a bank to place its cash money in the hands of one so young…. seventeen was it?" …."No, sixteen sir," said I on one of his forward tilts, underlined by a creaking noise. He altered his looking to my grease black fingernails, said…. "I'm sorry…. I'm sorry," loud over my pleading. With his soapy hand on my shoulder, he saw me through the doorway, watched me off, clear of his premises.

Chapter 24

The Southern Kain's side stayed as that terrible day had left it…. till spring. Only then did the dirt yard get fitted up by nature in a dress of weeds; only then did the black scar where the Kain's house once stood, wear green at places. The land was healing. It was at this time a telegram, another from Miss Lorraine was delivered. 'BUY THE LAND NORTHERN BOY FOR FIFTEEN THOUSAND DOLLORS, OR SEE IT SOLD AT AUCTION ON THE FIRST DAY OF MAY stop.' My mood was heavy, for the first of May was only two weeks off. I sat amongst new grown weeds, the beauty of the fresh spring day unnoticed. There was a Carolina wren, one I had often seen, perched on the steering wheel of a wreck; a wreck starved of color, a wreck with empty headlamp holes, just as if a skull…. that wren stared her black eye on me for a good long bit. In her beak, she bore a piece of brown palmetto fiber. She flitted like a blown brown leaf, into the left headlamp hole of this same skeleton wreck, soon to flit away. Her nest half-built, I could see there, bits of plastic, twigs, palmetto fibers neatly sewn together. My breathing stopped as I saw, built into that nest side half the head of Ulysses S Grant, upside down, giving a powerful stare…. there before me a scrap of a fifty-dollar bill! It took more than a few breaths to understand what I saw…. that Carolina wren knows where our Ohio box money is! Right here somewhere, but where?

When Eli saw me dodging, diving, hiding amongst wrecks, trying to keep that tiny spirit wren in sight, he shouted, "You sure got spring in your hydraulics boy! …. What you up to boy?" he followed me with a smile, eyes sparked in question. "The money's here Eli, somewhere the money's here!" I showed him the half-built nest. "PRAISE THE LORD! Don't that beat all of everythin', I've heard of puttin' money into bricks and mortar boy, but looks like we be investors in twigs and palm-cloth! If that money is here boy, I'll be caned in Hell-fire for thinkin' such bad about Snake Kain."

Our days were now spent chasing that Carolina wren, as she fitted, darted, danced from wreck to wreck. We scrambled, we hid, we watched from every fender, from every trunk back. We had cuts, we had skinned-off joints, we had deerfly bites lost count of, and the knowledge of every twig and leaf that that wren carried in her beak.... but she would not give up her secret to the black man and the northern boy.

It was Sunday, I was alone, in despair, only three days left, the Southern Kain's land, this land haunted by memories of Roxella, this land I had suffered on, would be auctioned to the hands of strangers. A fierce, beautiful voice fired across me and across the land, that Carolina wren. It was as if she taunted me, anger fired up in me enough to smite my fist on a car hood. She darted as if a glint of brown light, into a pile of tires. I ripped the tire pile apart, only to see her fly away. Now before me lay my Ohio box, tipped to one side, rusted lid half-open. Amongst muck, my five cent coins lay scattered out.... silver stepping stones; there inside the box, frozen, terrified, a big gray cotton rat guarding four pink babies, and those stub-tail babies, with shut eyes, lifted their blunt heads in trembling lifts, laid as they were in a nest of ripped $20, $50 and $100 bills. I have never seen a sight so straight motherly, as that gray rat mother, guarding her children, but the sight of my own mother's picture, lying in mud, chewed by rat's teeth exploded my anger. I came at them with a piece of pipe. The mother in her gray coat, went out, went back, covered her babies with her body, flinched there, her dark eyes fixed, the tip of her nose questioning air. I banged hard on the box, she ran confused, leaped, vanished like gray smoke, her babies motherless. I shook those babies from their expensive paper home, onto the damp, scraped up my five cent coins like a thief; gathered the shredded bills

like a robber; lifted my mother's picture, soaked wet, torn,
like a son, and left those poor pink babies to live or die.

As I sat then, gaining calm, an after-sadness came. I went
back to help those sad babies, it's then I saw that gray rat
mother, miserable, frightened, but bravely she came. Using
her mouth, she picked up a pink baby by the back of its neck,
carried it off, and each she carried that way, out of harms
path. Under where my Ohio box had laid, I saw, near-
buried, the knife my father had given me, now rusted; by
it, the acorn from our garden tree, that acorn had sprouted,
thrown a root toward the alien muddy sand.

Chapter 25

Eli had a dark level to his speaking next morning early. "If it weren't for my blind-eyeing that tire pile, on account of my rat fearing yellow streak boy, you'd have had that cash money in your grip two weeks back, as it is, times about out on it. I'm in shame double boy, for laying the blame of thieving on that Snake Kain. If you lose this land now boy, I won't never live it out of me." We both looked to the ground, till I said, "It's not done yet Eli. If we're quick we can get this pile of ripped up cash patched and to the bank, then a telegram off to Miss Lorraine Butcher-Kain."

The cashier handled each taped-up note by her finger ends, neck back, due to a thick smell of rat. The telegram I sent Miss Lorraine offering $10,000 cash got no reply. So it was that on the next morning, Tuesday, as the light came up, the entranceway to the Southern Kain's was filled with bidders. From the start, worry had me, the bidding went fast, I put in our bid….then a long gap, we thought we had it, till one more bid, then another, till $14,800 was reached. Our hearts drained, Eli laid his hand on my shoulder, as the land was knocked down to The Northern Top Soil and Fill Dirt Company…. the land was to be violated, ripped open, dug, trucked out for top soil and fill dirt.

It was within noise and sight of machines at the Southern Kain's side, that Eli and I now worked, as wrecks were trucked off. It was as if all our history was to be scraped clear, the land made ready for this violation of its body. Miss Lorraine Butcher-Kain, has sold her punishment onto the land. The old sorting platform was already gone, soon the parts shed, the scar of the Old Kain house, the powerful old live oak, along with the Old Buick, which still stood near to where it always had, soon all would be gone.

"There's somethin' strange," Eli said one morning as he arrived, "don't you hear it boy?" "I don't hear anything Eli." He slapped me on the shoulder.... "That's it boy.... THAT boy is silence! ....those machines is all standing dead today." As soon as we sighted the four-wheel drive truck with 'Environmental Agency' written, men boring samples of soil, we knew there just may be some problem. We learned from Clay, the land was found contaminated by oil and gasoline. It could not be dug and sold. Eli and I moved fast. We offered $10,000 for the land. "Look boys, I'm in no mood for jokes, from n****rs and juveniles, my job's on the line over this one, now get your 'asses out of here right fast," said the manager in our faces. It was only by a phone call confirming our bank balance that the land now at last, became our land and one land.

Chapter 26

"Remember boy, your first days here, I once said, 'We be cousins in slavery workin' for such chicken wages,' now boy we cousins in bossery," Eli said it with pride to his tone…. "partners you and me…. I never lived happier days boy, now maybe I should call you partner, partner in rust and grease!"

Within two years of our new beginning, our wealth had increased. We now stood before a newly raised-up Kain house. I had it built faithful to the original outside as well as in; even to the rough-made kitchen cabinets, old sink, table and chairs…. it really did look like a sister, almost a twin of the old place. Yet there was something in the bones of the old house that was lacking in the new, except the old chimney stack which had stood defiant as a fist, now stood proud as a chimney, against this new old house.

In the setting evening after work, Eli and I would sit on the porch, tilted back on wicker chairs, our feet up on the rail, staring out, bringing back past days and days better unremembered. One of these settling evenings, the last light dissolving onto the old familiar earth, stepped a familiar pair of feet…. Miss Lorraine…. from a stretch limousine. My heart lifted as the lowering black window showed Young Miss Roxella side-faced staring fixed forward. Soon I was helping Eli lift Roxella up the stairs and into her wheelchair once more. She looked pale, thin, but with a strong ghost of beauty still, it was hard to take my gaze off her. "What had spurred this sudden visit?" I asked Miss Lorraine as she quickly made herself at home by rearranging the knife drawer. "Why Lafe, we just had a yearning to breathe some of that f-i-n-e Caloosa river air…. You sure made a good job of a resurrection of a house, I feel quite at home. I heard that you and Eli are now partners," she said with one of her slantwise looks. I began to suspect that river air was not all that was chased by her nostrils.

Miss Lorraine was not usual in her dealings with Eli, she complemented his fine handling of the dish towel as he, under orders, dried the dishes that had piled unwashed in the sink. Eli gave a worried side glance, dropped a pan. "Sorry Ma'am'," said he. They banged heads as both stooped to pick it up. "Sorry Ma'am' I's sorry," said Eli. "Be a man Eli…. stop gaddam apologizin' for your very existin'!" …. Eli stood black-eyed straight-out confused, as Miss Lorraine got on with stirring the mashed potatoes with an unusually slow elbow. She shifted a soft look his direction, a look I could never think her face would allow. As well as this, Eli was sweet ordered, dog trainer fashion, to sit in the very place once occupied by Old Kain, at the table head. Eli sat on the chair edge at attention, as if on broken glass. Meantime, I was ordered to move my chair 'from Alaska, down the table to Florida,' next to Roxella, and almost touching. I felt blood rise, but Young Miss Roxella stared frontward, lips without blood, frozen there.

These were now strange days, "Miss Lorraine's bin syrup itself these past days," said Eli, his face up in quite a grin. "Can't get comfortable boy….syrupy, that's what she's bin…. like cough elixir….sweet on top, with a nasty under taste." "Seems like she's trying to dope you into falling for her Eli." "Na boy….couldn't be….she thinks of me as a black dog….always has."

I was leaning on the front porch rail, mist and moon before me, when Roxella, not managing the screen door, asked for help. She joined me there. There was the smell of spirits, as she said "Lafe," in a voice so thin and full of shakes, "I have to tell you the truth, we are without a dime, and worse. You remember Mamma sold her half to that dirt fill company, about two years back, nearly $15,000 she got. Mamma went on a rampage, spending, betting, buying every solid thing…. every solid cent gone! Gone to the dogs! I've learned much about my mother in these past two years…. I want no part in this Lafe. She's furious at me for not being buttery towards you. Her plan is, she will marry Eli; I will marry you; then after a fair bit of time, get divorced, take back half this place, she thinks is hers, in two quarter chunks. I was forced to this Lafe, my true bad feelings about my mother's plan I show in my coldness to you…. My true feelings…. well ….," her words were sunshine under the moon! "Roxella," I said, "the way I feel about you has only been held quiet by your iciness toward me. I still see that magical girl, flitting across the dirt yard, that pure white cotton dress, that electric blue waist-sash"…. "I'm far from that now Lafe…. far from that."

I moved close, she threw her arms, surrounding my neck, I kissed her nervous, short, my first ever kiss. Another kiss followed, stronger, that spoke all. "Dear Lafe," she whispered in a voice suddenly like a small bell, "Dear Lafe I don't want to hurt you. I must tell you I may never truly be able to love you or anybody. You see my heart has not died, it was never alive. I know you always cared for me, but there is just nothing there." "I…. I want to bring it to life." "I so wish you could Lafe." I asked about Luther, her eyes just blinked nervous, she said, "Luther was my way of hurting my parents with the most hateful thing they could imagine. I had no real feeling for Luther." ….There was a pause…. after another long kiss that alone I was lost in, we parted as her mother was questioning her whereabouts from inside the kitchen. And so in later days her show of ice was so well acted, at times I believed she truly may have a heart of ice. My only re-assurance was her melting in secret moments.

"You can bet on one thing, Eli," I said, "Miss Lorraine is after a piece of your shirt in this rust farm, guaranteed…. heard it from the lips of Roxella herself…. Miss Lorraine's desperate."

"Well, boy, guess she'd try to court a cockroach if she could get somethin'….what to do about it that's what eats at me, and that ain't an easy one…. she sure has turned her coat back-to-front. Should I play her along, get some more molasses out of her, see how far she'll go, or should I plain tell her I won't' be snared no how?"

"If you tell her you won't be snared Eli, she'll likely fly at you with one of those saw-edged knives she likes so well…."

"Be like throwing gasoline on Hell Fire!" said Eli. "It's just it feels like the edge of a sin to say nothin' boy…. but it sure is a turnabout, don't know if I can stomach it for long."

The sun sliced the kitchen end. Miss Lorraine stood half hidden in bacon smoke. Young Miss Roxella and I sat at the table, hands held under the table: Eli seated with us, well trained now by the boss of all things and people. Miss Lorraine skidded plates to Roxella and myself, while Eli's plate was lowered before him in a most civilized placing. Eli glanced at her edgewise and doubting. At once the door flung wide, such a flinging that pie pans and tin cups came off the hutch in a mad din. "WHAT IN THE WHOLE OF HELL?" yelled Snake Kain standing, legs wide a moment, swaying. He surged at Eli….ripped him out of the seat, holding him in a fist grip by his overalls. "I've a mind to kill you RIGHT NOW BOY, violatin' the place of honor in this house!" Miss Lorraine bolted forward, white knuckled, knife in hand…. "LEAVE HIM BE! …. THERE'S THE BOSS NOW!" she pointed the knife at Eli…. "YOU'D BETTER SWALLOW THAT PILL AND BE GONE!" "WHAT GOT INTO YOU BITCH, LOST YOUR BRAIN! …. PUTTING BLACK SCUM IN MA PA'S SEAT?"

There was an electric silence…. he cast Eli off, staggered to the door…. "YOU AIN'T SEEN THE FINISH O' THIS!" …. and kicking one of the pie pans in his path, then kicking a hole in the screen door to open it, he left.

Chapter 27

Eli and I ran Caloosahatchee Wreckers and Reclaimers well. The new sorting platform had been finished some time before, the old parts shed roof repaired. Clay and his truck were back in business, all seemed well on the scrap metal side of things. In the meantime, Eli humored Miss Lorraine, no more than that. Her syrup baited snare was failing. Young Miss Roxella did almost too well at the job of being icy towards me. It was at this time Miss Lorraine decided to take herself and Roxella back to Tupelo Mississippi, maybe to regroup her thoughts on the situation. And so, sadly I helped carry Miss Roxella once more down to the waiting limousine. I held her tight, maybe too tight, for when I finally released her, her hand was death-white. She gave me one warm flash of a look….and away they floated out of our lives.

Even though we were back in our old stride of working, my mind still haunted over Young Miss Roxella. The two new black workers we hired were big men, had big smiles that lifted my mood whenever I saw them. Their wage packets were big too to match. I took up my old working spot next to the sorting platform. The small saw palmetto I thought must be scraped dead to nothing, was still there with one defiant spike thrusting out from it's battered old body. Perhaps, perhaps there is still hope.

I received a letter from Young Miss Roxella, five days later…. it started….

'Dearest Lafe,

Continuing what we started can only lead to you being hurt, for as I think of you, I only have the warmest regard, but I will never be able to love you as you deserve. Please try to forget me. There are many better girls in the world. It is only for your own good I tell you this. I have never known love, so I can never give love, I will only scar your heart.

I will always remember you warmly.

Please Lafe, do not write back, I will not open your letter, this is final.

Roxella'

The wound of this letter left me in black loss, without hope. Her heart truly was never alive, never would it be, but how could I ever forget that magical girl? With this, a gray cloud was on me, on the whole place, as we were dragged back in time by Snake Kain. He took up his old ways and old habits in the parts shed.

He stood drunk before us, his overalls worn to holes at the gut, his pocket showing the worn outline, his last true possession, that old Civil War revolver.

He had taken on age these past years. He stood swaying, whiskey bottle to lips, how he got money for that….that, we never knew. He took two deep swigs, yelled, "What you monkeys doin' over this side…. Git, or I'll cause you to git! I'm come to take over this place, whip it back to somethin'." He staggered toward me, laid a heavy hand on my shoulder, more to stop the swaying than anything. Putting his face close-in on mine, with that smell of rot, said in as quiet a voice as he could get, "Put me in charge boy, put me in charge of these n*****rs, I know how to handle 'em."

The two black workers shook their heads, "No way, no way will we work under HIM."

Eli said, "There's no goin' back to before times now Snake."

"How about if I make you parts manager?" …. I said as his weight started to press me tilted…. "I ain't working under no blacks." He staggered off to the parts shed, muttering "Won't work under no blacks."

I peeped round the door, saw him lying there on the old collapsed army cot, gut rising and falling, under five molding rattlesnake skins still nailed upright there. He lay as if escaped back in time.

Under a lead sky, a gray Confederate sky, thunder sounding far off, Snake Kain staggered off toward the house, light was fading…. a single gunshot split the evening, a gray ground dove's wings whistled sudden skywards, Eli and I looked at each other shocked. In the rusted old Buick, bullet holes still in the door, we found him, fallen against the steering wheel in the last sleep; his hand gripped solid to that Civil War revolver, once used for the South by his Great, Great Grandfather Wade Kain.

Chapter 28

Only Young Miss Roxella Kain arrived for the funeral of her father Snake Kain, she was escorted by a Mexican maid. Miss Lorraine had decided to stay in Tupelo Mississippi, she had more pressing items to see to. Black shadows struck across the dirt to greet them as they arrived at the house that evening before the funeral. Soon Roxella and I were seated on the porch. "I was only able to come here Lafe, she began, since I hid away the last few dimes of the $15,000 my mother squandered." I told Roxella the story of her father's last days, how I felt bad guilt over it. She looked sad to her hands, cried bitter tears…. without lifting her head, she said, "It hurts deep to think of the life he had, if only a life could be unmade, made over, he would have chosen a different life, I know it. What he was, he was made to be by his parents, his place, his past. These things were beaten into him, they grew deep bitter roots.

I know you meant well Lafe, by offering him work but Southern Kains are a proud, stubborn race, I have adopted those same roots in me; for change is threat to us. When you and Eli rescued me out from the path of that tornado, I saw it coming, I wished then that you had left me, so I could have died with the world I grew with, was proud in, the way my step-father Snake Kain died. Now I have my life owed to a black man and a Northern boy. It is as if you have forced me to be born over, against my upbringing."

"I expected I would never see you again Roxella, I got your letter," I said. "In the saddest of ways, your father Snake Kain has given me a second chance. If only you would give us a chance." "Lafe," she said, "I am what they made me, the finest of education.... the poorest of love. I think when they adopted me after three years in an orphanage, my new mother wanted to re-make me into herself.... she more than did that Lafe. I am a Southern Kain bone and soul, I surely am! It's strange to think how I would have turned out if I still had my real mother. The only thing I have been told about her is that she was a prostitute, and glad to be rid of me, so I never tried to find her, for fear it was the truth. The irony of that is, that my new mother is now trying her luck as a high class version at the same profession, you might say, a business venture, along with her sister".... this news more than stunned me. "Who on earth would want?".... I said, but stopped short on that one. We both stared out at the silent moon a few moments, I let this new fact sink in.... then I said "Look Roxella, give us three months, if I haven't sparked your heart to life in that time, I will believe your heart is truly dead."

"You are blind Lafe, blind to my temper, blind to my moods, blind to my drinking, blind even to my damaged leg, you would have to take care of me. Lafe, one day you will open your eyes true, see, and cast me away, I know it."

"I NEVER WOULD!" I said, "NEVER!" Three months Roxella, three months.... "I will think on it" she said in a sad tone.

Chapter 29

Next morning, she sat in her wheelchair on the porch entry-way of that white painted church. I embraced her there strongly, openly, though it was as if I was doing the hugging for two. Eli, Clay and myself stood by her. She reached out, took Eli's hand. "I want to thank you Eli for helping rescue me, my mother, my father, out from the path of that tornado." Eli smiled his wonderful smile, bowed, said, "Oh Miss Roxella, what me and the boy did, it weren't nothing heroic." He gave two more bows, "I'm sure glad for you and that boy over there we did it," again he bowed. She put her porcelain finger to his lips, then to his shoulder to interrupt yet another bow, said, "But Eli I am not the only one who must try to change"

She now drew herself up shakily from that wheelchair, stood holding tight to Eli and myself. We walked, Eli straightened his old back, and proud we walked, and slow we walked, supporting her into that white-painted church, to the front where the coffin of Snake Kain was set. He lay as if in the parts-shed still, on the old army camping bed, five rattlesnake skins now across his chest. In the bend of his big arm that old Civil War revolver, bearing in the wood the notches of death, telling of it's part in the story of The South. We each placed a hand on the coffin edge, and there we stood, Eli, Clay, Young Miss Roxella and myself…. standing…. as I hoped we might stand again on some better day.

One hour on, at the grave edge, we looked down to that grim hereafter as Snake Kain was lowered. In silence we left, looking back once only to that lonely black hole in the earth.

The evening came inwards with violence, a gale hammered in, causing strange groans, shudders, creaks unnatural against the building corners. I slept disturbed, disturbed by the hot wild night, disturbed by the day.

I awoke in terror….a deep curdle-throat scream lasted a full-lunged minute….dropped to a terrible moan. I threw on my overalls, raced below, as did Eli. On the porch, in the early light, we found her….Roxella….face frozen, eyes in a horror stare….Before us, from the live oak, the body of Snake Kain hung by the neck on a slave chain, each shackled arm fastened outstretched as if a crucifix.

Under an evil sky….perched above….on a dead limb of that oak…. two vultures, greedy with hate, eyed the corpse…. his eye sockets already pecked to blood-black holes, staring to Hell. For bird, rattlesnake and man….revenge.

Pinned to his overall front….a notice….

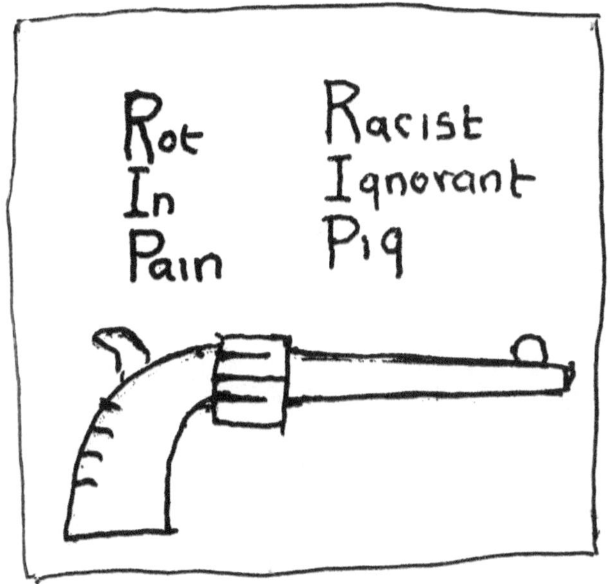